T0147400

WORLDS

Also by George Morrison:
Out From It All, Revolutions in a Lesbian Life

WORLDS

A Roaming Lesbian Goes Home Again

George W. Morrison

iUniverse, Inc.
New York   Bloomington

Worlds
A Roaming Lesbian Goes Home Again

Copyright © 2010 George W. Morrison

All rights reserved. No part of this book may be used or reproduced by any means, graphic, electronic, or mechanical, including photocopying, recording, taping or by any information storage retrieval system without the written permission of the publisher except in the case of brief quotations embodied in critical articles and reviews.

This is a work of fiction. All of the characters, names, incidents, organizations, and dialogue in this novel are either the products of the author's imagination or are used fictitiously.

iUniverse books may be ordered through booksellers or by contacting:

iUniverse
1663 Liberty Drive
Bloomington, IN 47403
www.iuniverse.com
1-800-Authors (1-800-288-4677)

Because of the dynamic nature of the Internet, any Web addresses or links contained in this book may have changed since publication and may no longer be valid. The views expressed in this work are solely those of the author and do not necessarily reflect the views of the publisher, and the publisher hereby disclaims any responsibility for them.

ISBN: 978-1-4502-2778-0 (sc)
ISBN: 978-1-4502-2779-7 (ebk)

Printed in the United States of America

iUniverse rev. date: 5/19/2010

To Irvin Goldstein, who is, in every sense, a teacher.

Chapter 1

Kera opened her eyes. Something was different.

The window curtains, jostled by the bedroom's tiny air currents, danced in a yellowy hue above the usually silhouetted brown table and blue shelves and dust particles shimmering like specks of gold in a miner's pan.

Before Kera's mind could assign meaning to this splash of color where darkness usually dominated, sounds from the kitchen of a chair scooting and her children talking confirmed that she had indeed slumbered well past her normal hour.

"Oh, my God," Kera whispered as adrenaline began surging through her, powering a quick rise from the pillow. "It must be nine o'clock," she said, now in full voice. She wiped the sleep from her eyes and turned to see the clock on her table. Its face flashed scornfully, "8:54."

"The New York Times. *The New York Times,*" Kera grumbled as she struggled to disencumber herself from the covers, awkwardly stood and rushed out of the room to find her children and her life's partner making pancakes.

"*Mar*ia! Why did you let me sleep this late?" a still groggy Kera asked.

"I thought you could use a little extra sleep, so I let you lie in," Maria answered, her northern German accent imbuing each syllable with precision.

"They'll be here in an hour!" Kera said.

1

"You've got plenty of time. I figured you'd do better in an interview with a full eight hours—especially as long as we worked yesterday."

"Well, that produce wasn't going to load itself," Kera said. "I'm going to shower."

"Are we going to be on the New York Times stream?" an exuberant eight-year-old Nathan asked as he stood near the stove.

"Maybe, darling," Kera answered, smiling at her son.

"Yes, you might, liebchen," Maria said as she monitored the frying pan. "They're coming here to write a story about Mommy Kera and shoot some video."

Kera made her way to Maria, caressed her black hair and kissed her gingerly, so as not to disrupt the cooking. She bent and hugged Nathan and his six-year-old sister, Sylvia.

"Love you two," Kera said. "Now I gotta get in the shower. Have a good breakfast."

After nearly a minute, the water stream still hadn't turned even lukewarm. So Kera, feeling pressed to be ready for the journalists, braced herself, then stepped into the arctic drizzle.

"Ugh, that's cold!" she said as her body resisted her mind's determination to hurry this shower along. Finally, the water warmed. Ten minutes later, Kera was motoring around the bedroom, procuring clothes, socks and a hairbrush.

She entered the kitchen in a striped casual shirt and blue jeans.

Sylvia swallowed a piece of pancake, then turned toward Kera. "I thought you already talked to the paper, Mommy Kera," she said.

"That was the Wellington paper," Kera said as she sat down. "This is the New York paper."

"Yes," Maria added. "It's in America where Mommy Kera is from. People all over the world will read this."

"People all over the world are gonna read about you?" a now wide-eyed Sylvia asked.

"They might. This will go out on the video stream and maybe in their print version, too," Kera said.

"Everybody at school read the story on the Wellington stream," Nathan said. "Our teacher thought it was real neat. So did everybody else, expect Andy Summer. He said it was weird to have two mommies and no daddy."

"Well, he's wrong," Maria said. "What counts is that parents love their children."

"And we love you two to pieces," Kera said as the hairbrush made its final strokes.

Thirty minutes later, Maria answered a phone call.

"Well, you need to go north on Route 1 about two kilometers, then turn left onto McKenzie Road. Then go two kilometers and a half. We live in a white, wooden house. Okay? Just ring us up again if you have more trouble."

Kera entered the living room after some final checking of her hair. "They lost?"

"Yes, they had the wrong road name on their GPS. But they're not too far away. They should be here in 10 to 15 minutes."

Kera's pulse quickened. "This always makes me nervous. That's the only thing I don't like about serving in space—all the interviews."

Maria smiled and reached out for Kera. The two embraced.

"I'm proud of you," Maria said softly. "You're a space heroine." She pulled back and they looked into each other's eyes.

"Thank you," Kera said. "But you're my heroine." They kissed for a moment, then started clearing the dishes.

Shortly, a car came down the road, something that happened only every 15 minutes or so at the busiest times. It slowed and pulled into the driveway.

"Okay," Kera said sharply, both to alert the children to be on their best behavior and to calm herself. Kera answered the knock as Maria stood nearby and two young faces looked eagerly at the visitors.

"Good morning. I'm Julian Ross," said a trim, brown-haired man about 40. He gestured to a casually dressed woman wearing a short layered haircut and carrying a small warehouse of video equipment. "And this is Jessica Bowen."

"I'm Kera McLain. Come on in." Kera introduced everyone else. "I'm sorry if you had any trouble finding our place."

"Not to worry," he said. "Hope we're not putting you out."

Something suddenly struck Kera about the reporter's manner of speech. "Are you from here in New Zealand?" she asked. "I thought you'd be from America. I mean, you work for the *New York Times.*"

"No, I'm a Kiwi. I live in Wellington. I grew up in the Taranaki province. I am a correspondent for the Times. I write many stories for them from here in New Zealand, but I'm not an employee of the paper or its online services."

"Same for me," the videographer added. "I freelance and do nine or 10 video shoots a year for American newspapers or streams."

"Gee, I was gonna ask how things were back in America," Kera said.

With that for a cue, the reporter switched on his recorder.

"Do you miss America?" he asked as the group sat down in the living room.

Kera felt a little cornered, but as she settled into a soft chair, she volunteered: "Sure I do. There are some things I miss about it all the time, like how cheap petrol is. Or gas, as we call it there. See, I'm not even talking like an American anymore."

Everyone laughed. Kera then offered the visitors some water. As they sipped, she continued.

"I miss my family back there, and American food. I know many people say American food is not so great compared to what you can get in other countries, but I miss going out for a hamburger or a pizza. There are carry-out places everywhere and the prices are so low.

"I mean the food is really good here, don't get me wrong. It's just more expensive, so you have to learn to cook. Maria knew more about cooking than I did when we married and I've learned a lot from her. We cook about evenly now," Kera said.

Maria, nodding in corroboration, added: "Yes, we're truly a female couple."

"Your marriage would not be legal in most of the United States," Julian said. "Is that why you chose to live here?"

"It's partly because of same-gender marriage being legal here, but not totally," Kera said. "We love New Zealand and we'd probably live here even if it wasn't legal. But that's something that makes me sad when I think about America. I don't know if it'll ever be legal there, at least in the whole country.

"And since people will be reading this all over America, I guess I'd like to say to them that, well, it's time for your country to grow. And I know it can grow because my family did. My father—and I asked him if it was okay to tell you this—was very hateful toward me being a lesbian when he first found out. But he changed over the years."

"Where are you from in the U.S.?" Julian asked.

"Louisville, in the state of Kentucky."

"How big a town is that?"

"It's got about a million people, but my family were basically country people who moved to the city. And you can't take the country out of the people, you know. That's why I feel at home here."

"It's 15 hectares of heaven," Maria said, prompting smiles. "We grow kiwifruit, radishes, spinach and several kinds of peppers and we sell them at markets in this area."

"Do you get away for pleasure?"

"Oh yes," Kera said. "We take our children into Wellington on the train and go to the children's theater and shopping and out to eat. That's always fun and the city is only 80 kilometers away."

"And," Maria said, pointing toward the east at mountains out the house's main window, "we've got the Tararua Mountains over there and the ocean to the west. We never run out of things to do when we get the time."

Julian shifted the focus. "Although you obviously like your life, it would strike many people as scant reward for your work on the Mars colony. I mean your work there was so above and beyond that the International Space Commission considers you something of a savior of the whole project."

"What's a savior?" Sylvia asked, immediately being told by her brother: "It's just like Jesus."

"No, honey, I'm not comparing myself to Jesus," Kera said, fashioning the comment for the journalists' ears as much as her children's. "The way he meant it is, somebody who saves something. I helped save the colony, but so did a lot of people up there."

Kera realized the children's presence was spinning the interview out of control, so she suggested they play video games or go outside. Nathan protested that "we want to be on the news stream," but the two sauntered to their rooms as both parents gestured toward the hallway.

"This is a lot of grown-up stuff that you wouldn't be interested in," Maria said as the two left the living room.

Julian asked age and other questions about Nathan and Sylvia, then returned to the main topic.

"I have never interviewed a space traveler before, but in preparing to talk to you, I have read many stories about them."

Maria smiled. "Not like the one Kera's going to tell you."

Chapter 2

Jessica shot video from many angles—gradually becoming less disconcerting to Kera. As Julian interspersed her words with questions, Kera told the following story:

I told you how my Dad changed and accepted my lesbianism, but he fell back a few times. Once was when I was visiting the family in Louisville. Maria was back in Germany, but I figured the best way to tell Dad that she and I were going to get married was just to come out and tell him.

So I did. Well, he hit the ceiling. He screamed, "Good God, they've turned you into a freak!" I'm not sure who he meant by "they," but it was obvious he wasn't as open-minded as I had hoped.

But the next day, he called me and we got together and he apologized and said he wished us well. I guess anytime something's new to somebody, they are scared of it. At least that's the way my father and his family are—most of my mother's family, too. That's the way most of America is.

That's why I'm glad to do this interview, even though I don't like publicity much. I hope maybe America will listen to what I've got to say. Europe, too, if they read the New York stream there, 'cause there are some narrow-minded people there, too.

They're not only anti-gay, but anti-woman. I've learned a lot about the feminist movement over the years. I never was political, but I guess I've come to see that I'm going to face narrow-mindedness and meanness, and you've got to organize to fight for your rights. I mean organize politically.

Also, I've learned that it's not just because I am a lesbian, but because I am a woman. That alone will cause some people to try to stop me from doing what I want. Knowing this has made me closer to heterosexual women and people of color, like the Maoris here, who have been hurt so much, and blacks in the United States. I guess you might say I'm more sensitive to unfair things.

And I had seen plenty of unfairness growing up. My two years on the Nova space station were during a time when I had no contact with my dad and not very much with my mom. When I came back down, Dad said he was feeling better about me being gay and feeling bad about the way he had treated me—throwing me out of the house and not talking to me for those six years.

Just as things started to get better between us, I flew off to Europe to work with the ISC, that's the International Space Commission—I know how you reporters are about abbreviations. I lived in Bremen, Germany and I loved it. I met some wonderful friends and I learned all about the lesbian life in Germany, especially Hamburg, which is one, well, crazy town.

We'd go there whenever we had a chance. We'd see street theater and go into real fun nightspots and eat all kinds of food from all over the world. And we met lesbians galore. Hamburg was a trip, that's for sure, but I also liked coming home to Bremen. Bremen's much quieter, but also a big pro-gay rights town, and those things made it just the right style for me.

They call Hamburg the Paris of Germany. I told my mom that in an e-mail and that got things rolling. Mom e-mailed back and said it made her remind Dad that she had always wanted to see Paris—the real one, not the Paris of Germany. So they decided to take a trip there and we arranged for the three of us to meet in Paris, then come to Bremen, and everything seemed great.

I called Dad and said, "C'mon over. I'd love to have you visit me here in Bremen." I told them to let me know what date they were coming. That's when it hit me. I didn't really want him coming. As mean as that sounds, it was how I really felt. I just plain didn't want him staying at my place for a few days, cramping my lesbian style, and just right there on the phone, I told him so.

I figured he'd be mad at me for saying that, but—surprise—he seemed okay with it. Well, we started sending each other e-mails about the problems we had had—me talking about how hard it was growing up in his home, and him talking about how his family and church told him homosexuality is evil and how he had no choice but to follow them.

Well, by the time we met in Paris, we were ready to start talking about all this in person. After I met them at the airport— and I *finally* found them after riding around people movers and trying to hear flight announcements—we all slept at our hotel the rest of the day, but then we talked.

Maybe seeing Paris brings out better feelings in people, I don't know. But the three of us talked, and, especially my dad and I expressed our feelings more over the next three days than we ever had. We talked about the same things we did in the e-mails. But in person, it was so much better. I had never seen Dad that way. I really felt sorry for him because he had the whole family bearing down on him the whole time I grew up. He had always been bearing down on me, you see, telling me girls don't do electronic things, they cook and clean.

Now, for the first time, I saw that part of the reason he had made it so hard for me was because of the way things had been for him. And me telling him that I understood this made us more comfortable with each other. I really felt great about him coming to see me in Bremen and meeting my lesbian friends, Paula and Amy, who lived in the same building with me. I couldn't wait for the train to get to Bremen so Mom and Dad could meet them. You see, Paula and Amy had been so great to me since I'd arrived.

Amy was from Scotland and Paula from Germany. We hung out all the time. God, I miss them and all that fun we had. Well, anyway, I called them when we got to Bremen. Amy was at work, but there was Paula to meet us, with her wire-frame glasses, blue jeans and shirt with some kind of radical environmental message on it, standing next to my Dad, who just a few weeks earlier didn't even want to see his own daughter because I was a lesbian.

They were opposites—that's for sure. But they seemed to like each other and Paula and Mom sure hit it off, too.

"Kera has told us all about Kentucky, and that has Amy and myself wanting to go there," Paula said. Yes, she had talked about the fact that she and Amy were a couple. I had told Mom and Dad this by e-mail, but now they were face-to-face and that made me a little nervous wondering whether Dad, and Mom, too, for that matter, were ready.

But, on the upside, I was glad that Paula didn't also say: "And she told us how backward Kentucky is."

We ate dinner at Amy and Paula's that night and, again, I was wondering how long it would be before Dad would get uptight sitting there in their dining room with this big feminist poster on the wall right beside him. But it didn't seem to bother him. He was more taken aback, I think, by the food. It was Chana Masala from India.

"I'm still learning, too," I said, grinning at Dad after Amy had to say the food's name three times to get him to understand it.

"Wait a minute," he said. "Let me get my German phrasebook out. Here it is: *Es tut mur leed.*"

Amy, Paula and I giggled, then I showed off what little German I had learned.

"That's, 'Es tuht mir leid,' " I said, saying the German for, "I'm sorry." Yep, it was a big multicultural world out there and I had only a little head start on Mom and Dad learning about it. And I suddenly realized how unreal it was to hear Dad apologize in *any* language.

Wow, this *was* a new world. I mean, my dad being so comfortable around Amy and Paula—and not being uptight when we got a chuckle out of him mispronouncing words. That was different from a guy I always remembered being so worried to death about what other people thought of him and terrified about being the tiniest bit not normal.

For a little bit there in Bremen, I was wondering if I had landed in paradise. But it wasn't long till I learned that finding paradise takes never letting your guard down.

Chapter 3

Mars called me—I mean I *really* wanted to go there, so as much as I would have liked to have stayed near Amy and Paula and Bremen, I accepted an ISC assignment to be a construction and robotics specialist for the first Mars colony. I had to move to England and that meant saying goodbye to them and their beautiful cat Tanner, and I think all four of us—yep, even Tanner—were crying when I left.

I would spend three years training in a center the ISC set up in buildings it leased from the U.S. and Royal air forces in Hillingdon, England, on the far west side of London. The U.S. and U.K. operate a base there called Blenheim Crescent. Both the air force part and our part of the base were offices and research centers—no flying, so it was pretty quiet for an air force base.

It was pretty around there, too—lots of green fields. It was just outside the developed part of London, but right on a subway line into the city; they call those "tubes."

Going into Central London for the first time made me miss Amy and Paula even more 'cause it reminded me so much of our trips to Hamburg and Berlin. London really swings and, like Germany, it had people from all over. It was like going around the whole world in just one hour or so.

But the truth is there wasn't much time for having fun in the city. We had long days of training and lots to study most nights. I trained in construction and robotics techniques for the colony Asimov they planned for us to build on Mars. They had a contest to name it and several people suggested naming it for Isaac Asimov.

The first nine months of our training were in roof construction. On Mars, we'd build a domed roof, as you probably know, by assembling flexible, rubber-like portions after we'd roll 'em out like a tarp on a baseball field. We'd raise the roof by inflating it with a mixture of gases—just like blowin' a bubble. Then we'd inject hardening agents into the roof to harden chemicals in it so the roof would be firm. This had been done in stadiums on Earth, but on Mars, it would have to be super-firm, 'cause there are 640-kilometer-an-hour windstorms that happen all the time and dust storms that happen about every two Earth years.

Through all this, that roof would have to perform perfectly; it had liquids that would circulate to even out the heat from the sun. I mean it was almost like a living being, that roof, and we really were determined to do it right.

As I said, we were always pressed for time, so for lunch, I'd grab some food at the base cafeteria most of the time. Well, one day the soda machine wouldn't take my money, so I asked the guy behind me for change. He didn't have enough, but he said I could borrow a bill from him.

I thanked him and said I'd pay him back tomorrow. He said, "Now let's talk about the interest." I smiled a little, then took my drink out of the machine and figured that would be all I'd see of him, except for paying him back. But he sat down at my table and said something that was like an old awful song I hadn't heard in a long time. I hated it.

He said, "No, seriously, you need to show some *interest* in me," then introduced himself as Seth Lowell from Southampton. This guy was thin and had short, light brown sort of wispy hair. It looked like what a rock and roll star might have worn 60 years ago. He had a couple of dimples, too. Put a leather jacket on him and he could have been in Liverpool way back when. It was the kind of look that heterosexual women might swoon over, well, at least till they heard his cocky mouth. Even most straight women, I hope, would be off board as soon as they heard it and I absolutely didn't like his style from the start. I frowned at him and moved my hand like, "No. Go away." But he said, "No, you see it's in your interest to show some interest in me."

I just kept looking straight ahead, determined to make no eye contact, and I said: "Maybe you didn't understand me. Leave." I pointed away from the table.

"Look," he said, talking a little softer this time. "You've misunderstood me. I'm not going to rape you, or anything."

"Damn right you're not!" I said, now looking right at him. "I took self-defense lessons and I carry teargas, and I'll spray you or any man who attacks me or looked like he was going to attack me. You got that? That stuff'll have you down on all fours coughing and spitting up like a…"

"Hey, cool it," he said, putting his palms up and scooting back in his chair. "I said I am *not* a rapist. You're acting like I said I was."

He sounded less cocky and, thinking back, I probably had gone a little overboard, but I told him, "You're the one who used the word first and I don't like people who use that word quickly, so just run along, even if you're not a rapist. I don't like you and I absolutely don't want to get to know you."

Of course, I could have told him the total reason I wasn't interested in him, but that was none of his business. Besides, even if a woman is straight, when she says "no," that's it.

For a couple of days, Lowell stopped bugging me, but then he sent me an e-mail that said he wanted to apologize in person and explain himself. I didn't trust that not to be a trick to get me into a conversation, so I e-mailed him back and just said: "Apology accepted. No explanation necessary. Goodbye."

I hoped that would finally end this. But later that day, after he apologized in person and started to explain what he had done, I had to remind him of what my return e-mail said.

Then the next day, during a break in training, he was at it again.

"I really deserve the right to explain what I meant, but you just won't let me. When I said getting to know me could be in your interest, I mean it could really help you. That's all I'm out for—to help you, 'cause I really care."

That was it. I decided to go to higher-ups. So I told a Dr. Lemanowski, the supervisor in our department, that I had told Lowell many times I wasn't interested and for him to leave me alone and that he just wouldn't.

"He said it would be 'in my interest' to start seeing him," I told Dr. Lemanowski. "I took that to be harassment. Like he means I won't succeed in my training unless I do."

Well, Lemanowski in some ways wasn't a lot of help. He all but said he didn't like Britain's strong laws against sexual harassment. He said they made him have to get involved in employees' personal matters. But he said the law did protect me and he would enforce it and talk to Lowell.

So I guess I had mixed feelings after meeting with him. I figured I really needed the help of a woman, so I called Amy back in Bremen. She recommended a great website about how lesbians can deal with a straight man's unwanted attention.

It said we should probably not pull the "lesbian card" by telling them our sexual orientation to get them to stop. The point is, no woman should have to put up with a man who won't take "no" for an answer. The other reason was because many men won't believe us and will think we made it up because we're desperate, so it'll look like we're gettin' weaker.

Well, as I said, Lemanowski didn't exactly seem like his heart was in it, but I hoped his talking to Lowell would end all this nonsense. But this Lowell character just got worse; he said something to me while several of us were just standing by waiting for our trainers to come by and grade our work attaching cooling lines together.

"You know you've misunderstood me right from the start," he said in that same cocky voice. "Remember when I said it was in your interest to see me? Well, I meant it. It could really improve your life. But please just let me tell you why. You see…"

"Damn you! I've already complained about this to Lemanowski, and I'll go higher up if this doesn't stop. I mean it. This is not some sort of game!" Those last words I got from the website.

Well, if that latest crack by Lowell had me thinking that going to Lemanowski wasn't gonna solve the problem, my next meeting with Lemanowski made me feel even more that way.

He calls me in for a meeting, he says he told Lowell of my complaint and says Lowell denied I ever told him to leave me alone. He said Lowell told him the "in your interest" remark was "an innocent play on words that was misunderstood" and that—are you ready for this—the whole thing was "healthy flirting and it was two-way." I still remember how those words hurt me, like a meteor smashing me while on an EVA.

"That's a lie!" I said, not even realizing that I had stood up. "I don't want him to…"

"I know, Ms. McLain," he said. "I know what you've said. But I have to balance that with what he has said. As I have told you, Britain's sexual harassment laws are very strict and I wouldn't want to ruin his career over innuendo or a misunderstanding."

"There's no misunderstanding! I want him to leave me alone, so I can concentrate on my work and do the best job I can getting us to Mars. If he will just leave me alone, that's the end of it. His career won't end."

"Look, I've looked up the law and it says unwelcome advances are harassment, not this healthy flirting. And this business about 'in my interest' is intimidation. I have also gotten advice from a group," I said, stretching the truth a little, which was okay, considering what Lowell had done.

"A group. Would that be the group you were in on Nova? I see here in your file it was called Women-Identified Orbiting Women, or *WOW*," he said, drawing out the word "WOW" with his British accent like he thought it was a strange name.

"No," I said. "It's a group here on the ground."

"Well, that's encouraging," he said, "because I have read in Nova records that while you were in this *WOW* group, you were instrumental in getting a man dismissed from Nova. He was called Mahuron."

For God's sake, how did that ever get dredged up, I thought. "I didn't get him fired. He was fired for destroying the first solar panel array. That was a four-million-dollar crime he committed—on his own. And that has nothing to do with this. And WOW was a great group. We made life on Nova better for everybody."

I could tell what he was gonna say next and sure enough, Lemanowski told me: "I'm just trying to establish that there is no pattern at work, that is you having what start off as innocent encounters with male co-workers, then these gentlemen get into trouble over it."

"Well, there's not. That's totally wrong!" I said, wanting to finish that with something stronger than "wrong."

"Very well. I'm just trying to be assured there is no such pattern."

I left that meeting so angry and certain that Lemanowski wasn't on my side. I could tell he was suggesting that he would claim there was this pattern if I took this to higher-ups. I had never seen people like him in the ISC before. I mean, I didn't always agree with everything they did, but the administrators during my years on the Nova project had never made me feel so abandoned.

So I called the greatest person in the ISC, the person I just loved working with up on Nova and on the ground—Collen Springfield. What a guy. Half the time I could never understand what he was saying when he got off on some talk about the universe or God or, what's that word he used all the time? Sustainability. But I loved him. He'd do anything to help you—including fly to England from his summer off in Switzerland.

Yep, Collen was up there in Hillingdon the next day after I called and told him what was happening. I knew I had the smartest person in the ISC on my side and he really cared. Collen is proof we lesbians don't hate men—you know that awful lie some people say about us, that we hate men. After just a half an hour of talking with him in my flat in Hillingdon, I realized how much love I had for him.

He told me enough was enough from Lemanowski—the next step would be to file a formal complaint. So that afternoon, we went to the ISC's human rights compliance officer, a really neat woman from the Virgin Islands originally—I loved her accent—and got her to e-mail us the forms. Why didn't we just file it right there, I asked Collen. He just said we needed to discuss all our options first.

I wasn't quite sure what was holding us back, but after some dinner, we went to this old, real pretty stone house in the country that one of Collen's relatives owned and let him use, and we talked and talked about strategy, including whether I should file a lawsuit or just a formal complaint.

At first, a lawsuit seemed like the right thing to do when I considered how much stress this whole thing had put me under, and what Collen said next had me even more for filing a suit.

"I know Chad Lemanowski. I worked with him in the planning stage for Nova," he said. "He is very competent, but he's a total failure in the human decency department. I'm afraid he has a history of pulling people into line by issuing reports on them claiming their work suddenly isn't good. I don't have the proof and it would take months of poring over files and talking to people to get the proof, if anybody would be willing to talk. But I'm certain that he does put out bad reports on trainees he decides he doesn't like, or that he considers trouble makers."

"Like me, if I file a complaint," I said.

Collen nodded. "It could cost you a trip to Mars. That's why filing a suit might make more sense. It would force the ISC to bring all this into the open and stop him from hushing you up with a bad report."

"Then let's do that," I said.

"Well, there's more, dear," Collen said. "A legal action wouldn't stay within the ISC, like a formal complaint would. With a complaint, no one outside of the people involved would know about this matter. But a lawsuit would…"

"News coverage," I said. "God, no."

"The ISC being such a visible institution with such an innately public purpose, it would draw lots of television and newspaper coverage—possibly worldwide."

"So I keep it private and Lemanowski bumps me from the Mars mission and ruins my work record, or I go public and the whole world knows about my personal life. You know me, Collen. I don't like news coverage even about the best things in my life. I sure as hell don't want it on something like this."

"Let's think about what other strategies we could try," Collen said. "I'd better make some tea. This is going to be an all-nighter."

Chapter 4

There was this nice-looking, tall grandfather clock in the living room and it rang real softly at 11 o'clock, then midnight, as we kept putting our heads together trying to figure out how to get out of this mess quietly, without the ungodly news coverage I couldn't stand the thought of.

One of the rules on the printout the officer gave us said I could not talk about this complaint with anybody outside the ISC–anybody at all, not even relatives or friends—or the whole complaint would be dismissed. It said if I told the news media or some political organization I would also face disciplinary action and I am sure that would mean being bumped from the Asimov project.

"I feel trapped," I told Collen as we sat there sipping tea. "I've never felt so alone."

Suddenly, when it looked like we were at a dead end, Collen got one of those looks like he had just figured something out—I imagine he's gotten that look a lot in his life.

"Alone?" he said. "You may have just led us to the alternative way to do this."

His hand went up to his chin. "If Lowell is doing this to you, he surely has done it to other women in the ISC. There's strength in numbers. Now we have to find these people."

"How?" I asked as Collen was pulling out his pocket desk top and

unfolding it. In seconds, he started looking at ISC personnel records, which he had the access code for and was allowed to see.

"I'm sorry, but most of these documents are off limits to you and it's important we not jeopardize our case," he said. But I could hear several "ah-ha's" over the next few minutes that told me he was finding helpful stuff, though what, I didn't know.

I don't know how he found it, but Collen gave me the name of a woman who had left the ISC four months earlier and said she might be living in a city in the western part of Canada. It was about 8:30 p.m. there, so I looked her number up. I can't tell you her name 'cause she wouldn't want it in the news stream or the paper, but I'll call her Susan.

At first Susan said she had had no problem at Blenheim Crescent, but when I asked her to tell me—if she didn't mind—why she left the ISC, she was quiet for a couple of seconds, then said, "I don't know, I just wanted to look for opportunities elsewhere."

I asked her what she was doing now and she said she was still looking for jobs. It was clear there was more to this than what she was telling me.

I asked her if she had had any dealings with someone named Seth Lowell. She said, "No," sounding a little annoyed. Then Susan said she didn't really have time to talk and had moved on from the ISC and would just as soon forget it.

So she hadn't told me anything useful, but she also had, if you know what I mean. It was obvious she had been forced out and this made us want to keep on digging.

At that old house, we made more calls over the next couple of days to people Collen got out of these documents, just like a magician pulling a rabbit out of a hat. On most, we just left messages and only a few were returned. Most of those people said they had no harassment at Blenheim Crescent—and these folks seemed like they meant it, not like they were hiding something, like Susan in Canada.

Then, one afternoon after my training session, Collen perked up while talking to someone, then put the person on hold.

"I think you should talk to this woman. She seems a little uncomfortable with me," he said. He transferred the call to me.

Again, I don't want to tell you her real name, but she had been an information technology specialist working on the Asimov project. She was from another European country and had taken a new job in Europe after leaving the ISC.

Talk about information specialist, she sure had some. It turned into a bombshell. She resigned from the ISC after filing a formal complaint against Lowell.

"Did a Dr. Lemanowski do bad reports on you?" I asked.

"Yes, he did," she said. "But that alone was not what caused me to leave. I had appealed Lemanowski's negative review of my work and I think I would have won the appeal. But then Lowell—he is the most evil man—he came to me and said something awful. But before I tell you, let me ask, what country are you from?"

"The United States," I said.

"Oh, well in my country we have a long history of respecting gay and lesbian equality but before I go on further, how do you feel about that?"

I was grinning thinking about how quickly I was gonna put her fears to rest. "Well, I couldn't be more for it," I said. "I am a lesbian and I just love what your country has done with same-sex marriage. I wish the U.S. would do that."

"Oh, I see I am talking to a friend. Then you'll understand what he put me through. Lowell told me he would tell the lesbian-feminist group I am in that he and I were having a love affair and that I made up the sexual harassment claim as a cover story to protect my reputation with them and all the other lesbians who have been important in my life.

"First off," she added, "the lesbians I know would not believe that and would not throw somebody out because they turned out to be bisexual anyway. Still, the thought of him saying that and people maybe for a brief moment thinking it might be possible just sickened me and had me so upset I could not sleep. I could not get my work done. That, with Lemanowski's report saying my work performance had become poor and knowing I would have to fight him, made me just give up. I couldn't fight both of them and do all the work required by my job."

"I see what you were up against—and what I'm gonna be up against," I said. "You see, I'm about to file a complaint with the ISC because Lowell won't leave me alone. Let me ask, would you write this down and let us include it in the report? Collen, that's Dr. Springfield—he's the man you just talked to—well, he said if I can get a couple of other people to tell the ISC what Lowell has done, they'll see he is acting wrong, that this isn't just innocent flirting, which Lowell claimed it is."

I had a hard time convincing her to even let Collen hear this on the speaker, much less to make a written statement. Collen and I both made it clear that this would just be an internal complaint, that it wouldn't get out, and that we together were stronger than the whole ISC.

She kept thinking about it, going back and forth over whether to get involved. She said she'd call tomorrow, and for a while I figured we'd never hear from her because she was so scared. But when she called the next day, she said: "We just can't let him keep doing this. I'm faxing you the whole story."

She did and with each line of it he read, Collen smiled wider and wider.

"It documents how Lemanowski thwarted her, not just what Lowell did," he said. "It says he suddenly started making bad reports on her work performance after two years of perfect evaluations. Our case just got a lot stronger."

Now if we could just get Susan in Canada to open up, he said, we'd be ready to win this fight.

I rehearsed a couple of times how to talk to her, since she had been so scared the last time. When I reached her the next day, she was still unhappy, and talked like *I* was harassing her.

I said: "If you could just let me send you an e-mail—look I'm in the same situation you were in and with enough people speaking up, we can win." I told her this taking it for granted that she had been harassed, too, even though she had never actually said that.

She gave me her e-mail address, but made no promises. So Collen and I worked on as persuasive an e-mail as we could come up with, with me using my knowledge of what it is like to be a woman at Blenhiem Crescent facing Lowell every day, and Collen knowing all the words he does.

She called me at my flat the next night and asked me: "Now are you sure none of this is ever going to get out to the newspapers or TV?"

"Positive," I said—and don't worry, I cleared it with her to let you put this on the stream. "The ISC rules don't allow us or the other side to go public at all, once the complaint is filed. And with your help, all we'll have to do is a complaint, not a lawsuit."

That apparently worked; we took the fax about four hours later at the stone house, which was becoming our mission control room. And the fax had everything—that Lemanowski suddenly told her her work was suffering and he said it sounded like innocent flirting—that's the same words he used with me.

"This makes a pattern," Collen said. "I think we can get Lowell sacked and maybe Lemanowski reprimanded—and you on the Mars mission. That's the most important thing, because you deserve it and we deserve to have the best onboard."

And two days later, when we filed that complaint at the human rights office, it had the statements from Susan and the European woman, as well as mine.

"Misunderstanding, huh?" I thought as the officer scanned those pages in. "All right Lemanowski, it's not just my word against his any more, is it?"

Collen signed on to become my advocate in the hearing, which would be done over two sessions. During the first one, Collen and I sat at one side of the table, three ISC officials were in the middle and there were Lowell and Lemanowski on the other side with no advocates.

I guess they figured they didn't need any. That sure changed when the clerk handed all of us copies of my complaint. In fact, they were told to forget an advocate, go for a lawyer, or solicitor, as they call 'em in England.

After telling all of us to keep this strictly inside this room, the hearing officer, Dr. Halloran, a woman about 50 with an Irish accent, said: "Mr. Lowell, I advise you to contact a solicitor. This complaint contains very serious and well-supported accusations of misbehavior by you while performing your duties with the ISC.

"And Dr. Lemanowski, the evidence is strong that you mishandled the situation. You also should seek legal counsel."

I mean it was like watching a giant go over a cliff. I could almost hear the thud.

"We'll continue one week from today," she added. "I remind all parties to strictly abide by the rule of confidentiality. There must be no discussing any of this with anyone not involved in this case."

I didn't look at Lowell or Lemanowski as we left the room. I'm not a rub-it-in kind of person and, besides, I was going to have to work around these two for the next week.

I don't know how they took it, but Lowell didn't talk to, or even look at me during the week. It was the most enjoyable time I'd had in a long while. I was able to concentrate on my training and studying, not on fighting off this wild boar.

In other words, I was doing just what a person was supposed to do who was training to go to Mars. And I felt like I was a person again. On Tuesday afternoon, after arriving home, I sat down at the computer, feeling relaxed and wanting to send some e-mails to friends all over. Then a call came in from the Lavender View, a great weekly LGBT newspaper I had read many times.

I had no idea on Earth why they would be calling me, but a woman who said she was a reporter there asked to speak to me. I'm afraid what she said spoiled my great mood.

"Ms. McLain, we received a printed news release from you about your complaint of harassment by a co-worker at the International Space Commission training center at Blenheim Crescent," she said. "I'm writing a story about this case for our on-line version that comes out tomorrow and a hard-copy issue Thursday and I'd like some information and comment."

The only comments I could make were ones she couldn't print. The second hearing session was in two days and if this story came out, I'd be ruined. I'd probably be bumped from the Mars mission, and even if I weren't, Lowell would be going with me. Me and him in the same ship for months with him feeling even more like his harassment was okay because my complaint had been dismissed—God, that thought made me want to puke.

I begged the reporter not to print the story and said I'd explain later. The worst part was she said the news release was signed in ink by me. She sent a screen shot of the signature and, sure enough, it looked like mine.

"I swear I didn't sign it or write it! Look, just wait a day, okay?"

Next I was gonna call Collen to tell him this wonderful news, but before I could, a call came in from the hearing officer, who told me to come in at 9 a.m. tomorrow for a special session. I could tell she had heard from this paper, too. Collen then called, saying the officer had told him the same thing.

"All hell's broken loose—and just when everything was going great," I told Collen, explaining the whole mess.

Collen is usually on top of everything and calm as can be, so I waited for him say something that would put my fears to rest—something that would get my heartbeat back to a normal rate.

And I don't mean just an "everything's gonna be all right" speech, but something that would lay out a plan to fix this mess.

But he just paused, then said, "Good God."

Collen, saying nothing more than that? Only then did I realize how much trouble I was in.

Chapter 5

After staying quiet for more seconds than I ever remember, Collen said, "Well, it's obvious Lowell and/or Lemanowski sent a news release to frame you and get the complaint dismissed, because they know they can't win.

"All right, here's what we should do," he added, now back in his usual style. "I've got a data scanner that can possibly trace a photocopy to its machine. I'll go into the base and check all the copiers he or they might have used and, I hope, find proof that one of them made the copy. But, on the other hand, they probably left the base to produce the copy at some store, so we'll have to search. How 'bout we meet at the Hillingdon tube station at six o'clock. We'll ride into the city and check copiers near this Lavender View office. It may be a needle in a haystack, but it's all we can do."

Collen's search of the base copier data turned up nothing, so we went on the underground. On the train, we talked over strategy while going under all those cool neighborhoods—Soho, Chinatown—and I wished I could just get out and have fun. But this was anything but a fun trip.

"Maybe we can convince Dr. Halloran you didn't write the release even if we don't find the proof," Collen said. "I'll call her. She's always been fair-minded and I know she thinks a lot of your work record."

But that didn't do it. After he talked to her, Collen turned to me. "She said she's tired of this whole thing, that it's distracting everybody

28

from our work, she saw the signature and we've got till 9 a.m. tomorrow to prove somebody else made the news release, or she's inclined to dismiss the complaint. We've got to work fast."

We stopped by the Lavender View office, where nobody remembered what the person who brought the release in that morning looked like. But at least we could see the paper it was printed on, and Collen compared it to samples of office paper he brought from Blenheim Crescent. They were different, so we headed out to office supply stores nearby.

At the first place, just two doors down the block, Collen introduced us as being from the ISC, which was the truth. We showed our ID badges and he said he needed to check for evidence top-level ISC administrators needed for a hearing tomorrow, which was also the truth.

When the manager asked if this was related to fighting terrorism, Collen said yes, indeed, it was, which was, well, close enough. I mean, hey, we weren't the real liars. Those were Lowell and Lemanowski, who were sitting at home drinking lager, watching TV and smiling at how they had pulled one over on the ISC and us.

So she let us check the copier machines and my palms were sweating waiting for Collen to do another "ah-ha," but after a couple of minutes, he told her thanks for her trouble and we left for the next place, which was a block and a half away.

There, a much busier store, we had to go through two managers, then talk to the regional manager at his home by camera phone.

"Now why do you want to check data from our copier machines?" he asked. "I don't understand and I don't see what business you have probing people's copies."

"Sir," Collen said, "the success of the first mission to Mars may well depend on you letting us scan the machines."

That Collen.

"Well, our firm's privacy policy is that no one can see residual data from other people's copies. That is the personal business of the person who made the copy."

Ah-ha—now it was my turn to say that. This man had said, "other people's copies." So I jumped right in.

"Sir, we're looking for my copy. I'm the one who made it," I said.

Collen, thinking for a second there that we were still arguing our case before Dr. Halloran, said: "No you aren't—*Yes you are!* Her signature is on the copy!"

He then convinced this guy to let the manager in the store use the data scanner and see if a copy had a signature that matched the one on my ID badge.

We nearly died of anxiety waiting for her to say something as she went over the day's data, going from the first copier to the next one. Suddenly, she asked for my ID badge again. She looked at it, then at the scanner screen.

"Yes," she said. "The signatures match."

I couldn't believe it. Lowell had outsmarted himself. If he hadn't forged my signature, we would have been sunk. She let Collen download not only the image of the news release, but the time and date it was copied—that was 9:52 that morning.

Then she let us check the record of the sale at the terminal and, apparently now on our side, called a morning clerk at home, who told us she remembered a guy matching the description of Lowell we gave her. She said he wore gloves, something unusual this time of year, so it stuck in her mind.

And, yes, since we were on a roll, this woman agreed to fax Collen a signed statement saying this. God, were we tired, but feeling okay riding the tube back to Hillingdon.

I slept well and I was never so happy to get up early to go to work the next morning. Collen called and said he had received the clerk's fax. That news got me really juiced up and an hour-and-a-half later, we presented the fax and the copier data at the hearing.

I still remember the words in that clerk's statement, cause as the hearing officer read them, I felt like I was freer and freer: "I sold a single copy in cash to a man about age 30, five-foot-ten with short wavy brown hair, light brown, really, this morning, August 14, at 9:54 a.m.—that's the time on the Point of Sale terminal. I remember him well because he was wearing gloves, which is really unusual in this weather."

"Gloves to keep his fingerprints off the paper," Collen said. "And the store clerk gave a description that fits Mr. Lowell."

Dr. Halloran turned toward the other side of the table. "Mr. Lowell," she said, "records show you were granted two hours of leave yesterday morning by Dr. Lemanowski."

"That," their solicitor said, "was done to allow Mr. Lowell to prepare his defense against these charges." The solicitor was a woman and I wondered how she could defend a man she must have known could easily start in on her the way he did me.

"Mr. Lowell, did you print this news release and forge the signature on it?" Dr. Halloran asked. Before he could answer, the solicitor asked for time to talk with Lowell and Lemanowski. The three left for a side room, where they stayed for 20 minutes. I would have given anything to hear what they were saying; maybe this solicitor realized what sleaze she was defending.

They came back into the hearing room, with Lowell looking absolutely blank—so different than I had ever seen him.

"Dr. Halloran," the solicitor said. "My clients no longer dispute the complaint. We concede the charges are true."

Wow. I felt like the world was lifted off my shoulders. Or maybe, it was that I realized I was gonna lift off. Then came, well, I couldn't believe this either.

Dr. Halloran said: "Mr. Lowell, my decision is to terminate your employment with the International Space Commission immediately, because you have egregiously misbehaved on the job. And, be advised, we will turn over any evidence we have to outside authorities for possible prosecution for forging a signature."

As if I needed more feelings of being on top of the world, she added: "Dr. Lemanowski, you are hereby placed on two-week unpaid leave while we decide what action to take against you. I assure you, you will absolutely not be brought back to Blenheim Crescent or the Asimov project."

They deserved it, I'll tell ya that. But I still felt a little awed that we had beaten two people who had seemed to have all the power. I wasn't feeling like gloating, or even angry, as we left the room. Then, as Lowell was getting on a lift, he spewed out his last ounce of trashiness.

"Well," he said, "you certainly made a lot of fuss over a chap asking a woman out."

That was so damn false that I looked around to see if anybody else had heard it so I could correct it. Nobody seemed to be in earshot, so I figured just let it go. After all, I had won all I had set out to win. But then he grinned in that god-awful way of his and said, "You lost me my job, but you're the real loser, know that. You missed the chance to change. You call it *harassment*. But what it really is is the cure for lesbianism."

"So that's what this was about, you bastard," I said. I wanted to break his neck, but I just looked him in the eye and said, just before the lift door closed: "Uh, uh! Lesbianism is the cure, pal—the cure for your type of thinking."

Damn that felt good. It summed it all up and was perfectly timed— the last word. I pounded my fist on my palm and looked at Collen, who nodded "yes" as we walked down the hallway back to training room C where I started making up for some lost time.

Chapter 6

At last, my mind was filled with circuitry and robotic configurations, not filing complaints, dealing with solicitors and racing around checking the copier machines of Central London.

Just like happened with the guy called Mahuron that Lemanowski had brought up—a guy you may know about 'cause it made news when he sabotaged the Lux 1 project up on Nova—I figured I'd soon be forgetting Lowell and Lemanowski, and I was till I was called in to give a statement to the police about the signature. I told all I knew and so did Collen and the copy store people, but there just wasn't enough evidence to convict him of forgery, so they didn't charge him.

Funny, that signature was what allowed us to get the goods on him and get him fired—without it, the ISC would have decided I sent the release.

Collen said Lowell's solicitor probably convinced him during that 20-minute meeting in the side room to admit to the harassment so the ISC wouldn't investigate it more and find proof that he did forge the signature.

In other words, he chose being out of a job to going to prison. Maybe he thought about it and realized that hitting on people works both ways and he didn't like the idea of *being* cured. Sorry, that was raunchy. I really do believe in respecting people, even people who pull what the Lowells of the world pull. A lack of respect going way back in their lives may have something to do with them being that way.

And I do hold onto hope that people like him can change. But I wasn't gonna stick around for that. And I had so much work to do for the Mars mission that I hardly thought about ole' L and L at all till I agreed to do this interview. From that point, it was all about Mars.

Damn, that was a beautiful planet. In the pictures we used in training, it looked liked the desert of California and Arizona I had driven through when I was an equipment installer just out of high school.

The training got more involved as we started working on environmental simulation. That was learning how to exist in our quarters on Mars, not just learning construction methods. For this, we moved into dorms full time and out of our off-base flats.

It was like Nova training again, except that we were just 32 people and we would be together for six months going to Mars, then two years there. The plan was for another group to join us in Asimov after we got it up and running. Then, who knew? They planned to bring us in the construction crew back after two years, but absolutely nothing was certain. At least for many months or a couple of years, we would see no one else except each other.

There was no moment when the whole world watched us lift off— like Apollo 11 back in the 1960s with all those thousands of people there and millions more watching on TV. We didn't all leave at once. We lifted off in several launches up to—are you ready for this—good ole' Nova. It was so fun to walk down those corridors and remember all the fantastic things we did back then.

The Novacom newspaper interviewed me and the other three Asimov project crew members who had served on Nova. It made me feel like a wise old veteran. I really did feel old for the first time in my life, telling them about all these people that nobody on the station remembered.

There wasn't much time for reminiscing, though. We boarded the Nerva, a craft propelled by a nuclear engine, with the fuel being ignited by the power of a controlled nuclear reaction. Some anti-nuclear activists didn't like building an engine like that, but it was the only way for us to get enough propulsion to get to Mars and back.

You don't just go "woosh" and go straight to Mars, like driving from Wellington to Auckland. You leave Earth orbit and go into a solar orbit and keep circling the sun till you reach the point where you can insert into an orbit around Mars.

It's like riding a merry-go-round. It took five and a half months for us to reach the Martian insertion—and that's with the mission timed with Earth's and Mars' orbits to make for the shortest trip possible.

The return trip was another five and a half months. It was very different—more on that later.

In just a couple of years, they'll start using a magneto-plasma propulsion system on test flights. It uses electricity and magnetism to eject plasma, instead of thrust from the fuel we use now. If it works out, it'll take just about six weeks to reach Martian orbit. But for us, it was the slow nuclear propulsion. Some day soon, it will seem so old fashioned, like an antique car.

Slow as it was, it never got boring on the TMSO. That's the Trans-Martian Solar Orbit. That's what they call the part of the trip going to Mars—I knew you were gonna ask what that stood for. We still practiced our construction and robotic techniques on computer simulators to keep us fresh.

Another thing that made the TMSO pretty lively was that the ISC set up transmission times when we could send e-mails to them and they would forward them on. There was quite a battle over whether the ISC would get to screen our e-mails. Collen and others wanted the ISC to forward them on without anybody in the organization being able to see them first, but the head honchos wouldn't hear of that. They figured all communications were the ISC's property.

Things like that changed my view of the ISC. The biggest reason I was more down on them was the fact that the only reason I wasn't cooped up with a sexual harasser was because of Collen and me running all over Central London that night. I would have felt better if the ISC administrators themselves had gotten rid of Lowell and Lemanowski but it took us, a couple of rebels, to get that done.

But at least we got rid of 'em. All of the 32 people in that Nerva ship seemed like decent people, not a harasser or a homophobe that I could tell.

I guess the best way to describe the trip to Mars is to remember *Treasure Island,* this great book I read in high school—not because the trip was like the book, but because it was *nothing* like it. When you think of the word "ship," you think of salty air, seagulls, rockin' waves—just like in the book.

But there was none of that on Nerva, not on this so-called ship. I'd have given anything to feel some ocean waves or hear a gull. We couldn't hear or feel a thing from the outside—of course that was good, 'cause if we did, it would mean we had been hit by a meteor and that probably would have meant bye-bye forever.

There wasn't much to taste either. Our food was pretty good, but it was mostly freeze-dried. We also had some fresh vegetables and roots from the hydroponic garden—that was the big area of plants grown in water. The plants made most of the oxygen we breathed, so you bet our two botanists were important to us.

They cared for those plants day and night, keeping 'em free of disease. We had only a couple of months of oxygen on reserve if those plants were to die in an epidemic, so, yes, we saved every seed.

The Nerva was a big cylinder with zero-gravity inside, but outside, about 200 meters from the cylinder, was a ring that three modules could be rotated on to produce artificial gravity. One was the hydroponic garden; it rotated all the time 'cause you've got to have gravity to keep the water in place.

Then there was the "Ag." That's what we called the Artificial Gravity Module. On the TMSO, it was set to create 38 percent of an Earth G by centripetal force as it rotated. That's one Mars G.

As we got closer to Mars, we stayed in the Ag longer and longer, until we were in there a few hours most days. It not only kept us from suffering the bad effects of months straight of zero G, it got us used to Martian gravity, so we wouldn't have to spend the first few days on Mars learning to walk again. And that was important because with those Martian winds of about 640 kilometers an hour—that's 400 miles an hour for the folks in America—and bursts of high radiation, we had to get to work right away building the dome.

Of course, how could I not mention that the whole thing, the Ag included, was encased in a five-foot-thick layer of lead? Yes, we needed that to keep us safe from the deep-space radiation that is deadly outside the Earth's magnetic field. Scientists believed the radiation could cause cancer and destroy our brains' stem cells.

But those lead walls could soon become a thing of the past. We did experiments with our own magnetic fields to keep the radiation away. We used superconductive electrical wiring systems for the whole ship to create a mini-magnetic field.

The Earth's magnetic field is what repels radiation so all of us can sit here safe and talk like this without worrying. Back then, we were a few years away from using this mini-field system full time for whole ships. They're using them now, but on our mission, we just experimented with it, using it for a few minutes a couple of times to see how well it worked.

We weren't ready to rely on the mini-field for real without the lead, 'cause if we did and it failed, we were toast. But we did use smaller versions of the superconductive systems while on Mars. They sent out magnetic fields from the windows of the Martian Excursion Module, the MEM—that's the craft we descended to the surface in.

Even though we were pretty confident with those systems, we had lead layers that would close down over the windows if the magnetic field wires failed.

And we used the same wiring system to send out a field from our suits we wore while walking on the surface. In case those failed, we took an MLS, Mobile Lead Shelter with us on our walks. We could get inside right away and ride back to the base.

But, as I said, we weren't ready to use the mini-field on the Nerva full time. So EVAs outside of the lead were out of the question. What does EVA stand for? It's Extra Vehicular Activity, complicated space talk for going outside the ship.

We did the maintenance on the outside of the Nerva by remote controlled robotic arms we maneuvered from inside, safe in the lead.

Because of those thick walls, almost everything we saw outside was by video monitor. We had only three windows and looking out them was looking down a five-foot-long tunnel through the lead. And those tunnels weren't open very often—only during low periods of solar radiation and for just a few minutes at a time, so the cosmic rays that are always out there wouldn't build up in us.

So there wasn't much of the breathtaking view you'd expect on a space mission.

Another way serving on the Nerva was different from going up on Nova was that back then, we lesbians had to find each other, and we did. That's how we formed WOW. This time, I knew the other lesbians beforehand—all one of them.

That's not to complain, though, 'cause Liz was great. Liz Dyer was her name. She was a scientist, a biologist. Her first job would be to make the Martian soil usable to grow our food.

Then after we got the colony fully built and running, she would do experiments to look for life forms on Mars.

And Liz and I understood each other, even though our schooling was so different—me with a vocational education and her with a PhD.

It wasn't just that we were the only lesbians onboard, we were American lesbians. She was from Maryland—Land of Mary, I used to like to call it, 'cause her full name was Mary Elizabeth Dyer. We knew what all the gay rights struggles were like in a country where the government, at least the federal government, was so against us. We both lived in places where local governments passed some gay rights laws. So we knew that in America, local government was much more friendly to our causes and that was as high-up as it was gonna go for now.

We both grew up in churches where the preacher, or the priest in her case, said, "homosexuality is a sin," and we knew that was a lie. Of course, they also said we should "love the sinner, but hate the sin." Yes, I heard our preacher say that and she remembered seeing that in a church newsletter.

"If gay is a sin, why would a god who is supposed to love us all make some of us gay?" I asked while we were talking after I finished practicing on a simulator one night.

"Bingo!" she said. "You hit it right on the head."

We talked from time to time about what God really is—not just the God in the Bible that is the God of Christianity only, but a God that is for everybody, of all religions and nations. And how God is more complicated than what any one religion says, because it is obvious that the Earth wasn't made in six days and it sure isn't the center of the universe.

"God is love—and truth," Liz would say, making it sound so simple. "Nurturing, caring love. And truth free of any deception."

While all the fundamentalists and scientists were supposed to be at war with each other, Liz the scientist's message was: stop the war. "Religion is religion and science is science. They are different ways of seeing the world and they don't rule each other out," she said.

That was also so soothing to me and it made so much sense, especially when you consider there were enough other problems in the world that religious people needed to pay attention to instead of fighting over creation versus science. Bingo to her, too.

Liz was in her late 40s and had wavy hair that was starting to go gray—she loved that; it made her feel more valuable because it told people she had experience and wisdom. It's pretty normal for lesbians to feel that way, you understand, at least for us feminist lesbians.

Liz talked with the neatest accent. I couldn't place it. On some syllables, it sounded southern, more southern than people in Kentucky even. Then, her words would come out northeastern, like the people from New Jersey or New York we trained with.

Liz told me that was because she talked "Delmarva." That's Delaware, Maryland and Virginia. It mixed the south and the east and I just loved it, maybe because it made me feel closer to people from the east, like we spoke the same language.

Anyway, in a place full of accents from all over, Liz's was unforgettable.

Chapter 7

Even though, as I said, the ISC screened all of our e-mail, they felt okay with *Proponent*, an LGBT magazine, doing a story on Liz and me and the whole Asimov project for print and online.

They transmitted a whole slew of questions to us, some by e-mail, some by video stream—by this time in the mission, it took about three minutes for them to reach us. We e-mailed back the written ones and sent a video back talking more about what we had done in our lives—that's what the video stream questions were mostly about.

Because that order that we not talk about the Lowell case was still on, I didn't mention it outright, but told 'em that I had come up against plenty of sexism and homophobia, then told 'em about the Mahuron case—about how this Nova technician from Ohio sabotaged the first space-to-earth photovoltaic system to try to make it look like it was my fault. Or as he put it, "to get rid of one of them."

I also talked a little about my family and how much progress we were making.

I still don't know whether the ISC monitored our answers to *Proponent*, but I expect they did, 'cause gay rights was still something that got people stirred up. But they didn't seem to censor anything; when the story came out, Liz and I both loved it.

The headline was cool: "Eve and Eve. Kera McLain and Liz Dyer will soon be the only lesbians in the world." That must have freaked people out at first, till they figured out they were talkin' about Mars.

Well, I e-mailed Paula, Amy and Collen about it. They sent up pictures of the hard copy of the story. I liked it, too. And that's really saying something because, well, don't take this personally, but I haven't always liked what the press has written about me.

That story talked about everything—our views on gay rights, my hanging out with a group called the Louisville Women's Circle back in high school. They were a great group of people and the story told how they taught me about feminism and religions that are not patriarchal.

The story also passed on some of the views that Liz and I had bounced off each other of God being love and truth.

And that got my mom to e-mail me that she was so happy to see me talking about God that she cried. That was nice—to see that my family and I could agree on something. I thought at first, just let it be. But I had to be honest and I told Mom, well, you know, it's nice that you said that, but I am talking about something very different when I say "God."

Then I told her how God isn't a man, isn't just the Christian God, and that those who think God is just those are closing their minds. God, I told Mom, is—just like Liz said—love and truth and caring about people. These people who say God hates gay people aren't worshipping any real god.

I braced myself, but she said that was fine, that I should seek God in my own heart—which was exactly as I would have put it, and I told her that. There we were, about 25 million miles apart and we were closer on that subject than we had ever been before. I mean we never talked about God before I was old enough to know I was gay. Then, I listened to all the anti-gay prejudice coming from the church when I knew I was lesbian.

I wonder why I keep having to go away from home—first to Europe, then to *another world*—to get closer to my family.

But back to the mission, Mars kept getting bigger on our monitors and the few times we could see it out the windows. It went from a little light to, well, you know, a red planet. Then we could see the white polar caps. Soon, it was as big as a thumbnail at a straight arm's length. And we started thinking about the approach and landing. First, we started getting the MEM fully powered up. That wasn't really my task, but I loaded equipment and supplies into the MEM, which would take 24 of the 32 crew members, including those of us in the construction team, down to the surface.

The landing site was in Acidalia Planitia, a mostly flat region in the northern hemisphere, between mountains to the east, west and south, and the polar region to the north.

We had timed the landing to be just at the end of the dust storm season; the storms get real bad when Mars comes closest to the sun. We absolutely had to have our dome built and running before the next storms, which could cover us. That would give us well over an Earth year to finish the dome, because a Martian year is 687 Earth days long.

Well, I don't have to tell you much about the landing because you probably covered it, or at least watched it. We fired that Nerva nuclear engine again to drop into a Martian orbit of 95 kilometers high.

Two days later, we entered the atmosphere—that's right, we didn't *re-enter* it. We were the first human beings to *enter* an atmosphere from space. And even though the Martian atmosphere is so thin, the heat shield on the outside of the MEM a few meters beyond the lead reached 2,700 degrees Fahrenheit—that's almost 1,500 Celsius.

I'll never get used to that much heat being just a few feet away. It's spooky. You can't wait to get through it. After the entry, at about 12 k high, we fired our engine. On the monitors, we could see that red atmosphere, but I couldn't help but think about how it was 95 percent carbon dioxide—pure poison.

We kept dropping, four meters forward for every one down, then one to one, then almost a straight drop. We were eight percent on bingo—sorry, that means we were approaching at a rate where we'd have eight percent of our fuel left when we'd land. That was a pretty comfortable margin.

Then we saw dust—lots of dust—and that meant we were almost there. Then we could see it—the contact light coming on on the control panel up front. Suddenly, we dropped a little as the MEM's legs absorbed our weight. All I remember next was Liz and me looking at each other, giving high fives. Although we were several meters away from each other, we could almost feel our hands touching.

I'm sure you know how people on Earth felt at that moment. It was one of the greatest events in history. But to us, it was also a little worrisome, because those winds of over 640 kilometers an hour were possible at any time. So we had to hurry and get lodged into the surface, and real deep. The MEM extended its five metal arms to dig in about three and a half meters, then smaller fingers extended a few decimeters more into the soil.

They were designed to keep us from toppling in a sudden wind, and a computer would adjust the tension on each side for the direction of the wind.

Once the sensors showed we were dug in enough and the computer was reading the wind okay, we could relax a little, although, really the word *relax* just doesn't describe it, looking at—what's that they call it—a brave new world. We mostly stared out the window at the richest, reddest soil you have ever seen.

We ate a meal that was great—burritos and nachos. Finally, we could eat loose foods like that. The chips and burrito filling would have floated all around the ship in zero G.

Then we were back in those windows like cats looking at birds. We couldn't wait to get out there. And I still remember exactly what Bruce said—that's commander Fanelli—when he stepped off the MEM. He is Canadian and it was quite a thing in Canada that he was the first. He said:

"I dedicate the first step onto a new world to all whose sacrifices made it possible. May our arrival on this planet inspire our brothers and sisters on Earth to cooperate, as we of many backgrounds and nations have done to come here."

That was a lot to think about. When he said "sacrifices," I figured he was talking about those who died, like in the two space shuttle disasters, and before those.

The one I thought of first when Bruce said what he did was Roger Chaffee, an astronaut who died preparing for the first Apollo mission. In this old video, he said he hoped to go to Mars. He never made it off the launch pad. He died in that terrible fire so long ago.

But here we were, partly because of his sacrifice, and the two other Apollo 1 astronauts, Edward H. White II and Gus Grissom, who was from not far from where I grew up. And boy, was I remembering them. On another part of Mars, there's the Apollo 1 Hills, with a hill named for each of those three men. It's nice knowing they aren't forgotten.

It was quite a moment when Bruce said that and took our first step onto Mars. Unlike on Tranquility Base on the moon, the footprint won't be preserved; the Moon has no wind.

I was dying to get out there and walk around, mostly because I hadn't been able to move around much of a distance for the last six months.

That soil looked so rich red—sort of like cinnamon—so I figured it would feel crackly when I walked on it. But the feeling wasn't as, well, lively, as I expected. It was just crumbly dust and my boots just sunk ten or twenty millimeters into it with each step. Sort of felt like walking in an inch of powdery snow, but the crunching sound wasn't as great, I guess because the atmosphere is so much thinner.

The sand was flat, except for a few waves in it a decimeter or so tall caused by the last wind gust. They looked firm, but they'd be gone with the next gust.

Just like we had figured in training, walking in 38 percent G was weird. With every step I'd take, it felt like somebody was nudging me on farther, because the effort it took to make one step on Earth would get you more than two here.

The electromagnets in those suits and the life support systems were pretty bulky and made walking awkward, especially at first. Truth is, those EVA suits were as much like a module we rode around in as a suit we walked in. I honestly was afraid we'd all look silly to the television viewers on Earth. But after a few minutes, I was more in control. Still, there was a cloud of dust a couple of decimeters high that followed me everywhere, caused by me bouncing on that surface.

And out there on the plains of Acidalia Planitia, that dust is everywhere. It's mostly small rocks there, not too many big ones, because the wind grinds 'em down. And just like in the training videos, it looked a lot like the desert southwest, except absolutely no trees, plants or animals. Not even bugs. There was no sign of people; it was just natural, except around our base.

I know many of you in the media complained that there wasn't much ceremony to the first EVA. But hey, we had work to do and we had to get to it right away because of that dust storm deadline.

It started when we dug out a foundation, then spread out four panels and attached them to make our first section of floor. In a little over an hour, we had made walls and a ceiling around the MEM. We put in solar electric, plumbing, life support, and *voila*, there it was—our home.

Back in the MEM, we answered reporters' questions, washed up and went to sleep. Finally we were tired enough that sleeping felt better than looking out the windows.

We woke the next day to a rude surprise—a crack in the window of the south wall. It drove home how dangerous this was; we could have lost our oxygen if we had already pressurized the place. Better that crack appeared when it did.

Well, we fixed it by spot welding a new window in place in about an hour. Then we de-pressurized the place to get rid of the Martian air and we filled it with breathable Earth air stored in the MEM tanks.

Then we really got going. A drone shuttle landed with supplies galore and the two best friends we had on this mission, Rosie and Nigel. Yep, I could see you smiling as soon as I started to say their names. You reporters were really tickled with those two robots and how much we liked them.

They worked fast and their work was excellent. We aligned them and typed in the codes and they did all the precise work, digging out ground, putting floor panels down, building support columns that would hold the roof up, attaching life support cables. They constantly built outward from the four walls we had built. They built in a circle until the construction reached the surface area we would need to put up the first dome.

There was a lot of dust from high winds, but it wasn't as bad as we had feared. Winds of 640 kilometers an hour aren't as awful as that number sounds when the atmosphere is only one percent as dense as Earth's. That doesn't mean the winds were a picnic—those gusts still knocked a few of us down once in a while and they blew some loose cables and other supplies away, never to be seen again.

The whistling sounds the gusts made while whipping past our suits sounded like tea kettles. That combined with the vibrations and tiny hum from the electro-magnetic wiring made it anything but peaceful out there.

Then, let me tell you about the dust devils. That's what they call the wind spouts that look like little tornadoes. They're caused by heat patterns that cause hot air to rise suddenly and they can make the air look brown or green for a half an hour or so.

They weren't all that much of a hazard—I mean just normal surface winds were worse. But they looked scary. The closest I ever got to a dust devil was about 70 meters, but I saw a couple of crewmates knocked down by them. They made me anxious to get our first roof up.

And after Rosie and Nigel finished building the first phase of those floor panels, the drones brought us what we called the big egg rolls—the roof panels we unrolled. That was a real miracle of engineering. I got to give it to the people who thought those rolls up.

We rolled 'em out like a tarp at a baseball game in America when it rains, attached 'em together so they covered everything, even the MEM. The top part of the MEM bulged out like a church steeple underneath the rolls. Then, we inflated the place with gas lighter than the Martian air. The whole thing rose and formed a dome.

What a feeling it was seeing that place turn into a domed building—a real place to call home with lots of room to spread out. But there wasn't time to admire it, because now came the tricky part. We injected chemicals called hardening agents to mix with the blend of jells and liquids inside the roof rolls and make them harden and expand. And there we had it, a dome—and in a few hours, after we verified that it was stable, we added a breathable atmosphere. The place was 55 meters in diameter and about 40 meters tall. Very comfortable, when you consider how little space we'd all had for the last six months.

After we were able to take our suits off, it was really fun to walk in .38 G. With no life support equipment on your back and no wind or dust, you could jump over desks and tables easily. And with a running start, I could jump longer than Olympic track stars. The first few days under that dome, we had to force ourselves to do our work.

But our work was so much easier now that we were under the roof. And I can't say it enough—that roof was so cool. Liquids flowed through it to even out the heat. It was just like blood flowing through a body. And this was just the first of three we'd raise. As we would spread out, we'd roll together a new larger roof—over the old one—then inflate it the same way. That's how we'd grow, disassembling the old roof each time. After the third roof was built, Asimov would be 825 meters in diameter, the size of a small town.

But that would come about 18 months later. For now, we started on the interior construction. That's not so interesting to your readers, I'm sure, because it's just like building on a construction site on Earth—it's a lot like the work my dad sometimes did for a living. We built rooms, walkways, an auditorium and a video theater.

The whole dome was a whirring, clanking, humming place with Rosie and Nigel doing their work and us feeding them supplies the fork lifts brought us—wall panels, utility lines, electrical wiring, atmosphere sensors.

Liz really showed her value to us, too. We brought in soil samples and she put them through chemical test after test. She lead a team using a whole lot of chemical processes to get the oxides out of the soil, then put beetles and earthworms brought from home to aerate it.

Yeah, we brilliant people with all our education were totally at the mercy of those worms and bugs. They absolutely had to do their jobs just like they would on Earth. But they had been born on a 100-million-mile trip, and now they were in .38 G, so we didn't really know if they would take to this soil just like they would have, say, here on our farm. But they did; I guess they thought they were at home.

Then Liz and her team did more chemical processes to put nutrients in that soil. It was complicated beyond my knowledge, but it allowed us to grow some of our food, especially grain—in our soil samples inside the dome, that is.

We were absolutely not allowed to change the soil outside this way 'cause it could contaminate it. I mean they had procedures to make sure we didn't drop a food crumb outside for fear that we could wipe out the Martian environment.

When Liz and her team started having success growing food in the soil samples, that was great news, because we had only a limited amount of Earth soil with us and an endless supply from outside. It also meant we had no problem growing enough plants to produce oxygen; we wouldn't have to rely on drones sent from Earth bringing us plants, which was plan B.

Water was our other big need 'cause there is very, very little of it on Mars or in the atmosphere. We solved that in a way that helped the Earth solve one of its problems, too.

We installed five different types of fuel cells, which create electricity. Some of 'em used alcohols, some hydrogen, which we brought from Earth. We didn't so much need the electricity 'cause we got plenty from the solar cells. But the other product of fuel cells is water. Yep, that's how we made our drinking water and did our plumbing, and what we learned from those different types of systems sped up development of fuel cells here on Earth and made them more efficient and cheaper. I'm very proud to have helped do that 'cause millions of people now get electricity from fuel cells with no pollution at all, partly because of our work on Asimov.

There was plenty of drinking water in the dome, but it was rationed for cooking and showering. Yeah, we'd start every day with a three-minute blast of shower water—we learned how to wash our hair real fast. Then we'd dry off, then go eat breakfast in the dining hall.

"Another day on the Acidalia Planitia," people would say while we were eating and getting revved up for the day.

If the water, air and food were about what we were used to on Earth, the calendar we had there was enough to drive you crazy.

As I said, the Martian year is 687 of our days long, and, would you believe it, somebody up there made a Martian day almost the same length as Earth's—almost. It's 24 hours and 36 minutes.

So they had a real tough time during the project planning deciding how we would figure our days—by Earth's clock or ours. They finally decided we would start and end the day based on our Martian time, then every 22 of our Mars days, we'd skip a day to keep the calendar the same as the one the ISC used on Earth. It was just the opposite of what we do on leap year.

It was crazy, but hey, I'm not complaining, 'cause it gave us 36 extra minutes of sleep every day. Not that we were sleepy-heads. We just shot out of bed every morning, the work was so exciting. After a month, we had a medical clinic up and running. Everybody had residences and we had a really nice dining hall. It was the nicest small town you have ever been in. And I was feeling real satisfied that all the studying, training and traveling were worth it.

Then, I suddenly was brought back down to—Mars, I guess you'd say.

We first knew something was up from the looks on the faces of the scientists. Every one of them looked worried as they came out of a meeting in a video conference room.

They would often look concerned, 'cause they had a million details to think of in their jobs. But this was worse.

Then, we kept hearing, overhearing really, talk about little thin cracks. Then we got the word that Bruce had postponed his weekly meeting with all of us and that clinched it—something was wrong.

There were no alarms sounding, so we knew those cracks, if that was what was wrong, weren't in the dome or the floor. Whatever it was, it wasn't a threat right now. Then Liz and some others got us to sign an e-mail demanding they tell us what was up.

So Bruce called us together for a meeting. I still remember every word he said; it was like a knife was going through me:

"There's a huge underground crevice about 600 meters to the east of the base and its tentacles are underneath the base's eastern edge. It's growing at an undetermined rate in our direction and will eventually undermine the whole station. It's too complex and big for us to fill with dirt. Besides, dirt likely won't stop it. The size and complexity of this thing indicates it will just re-expand."

The more he told us, the worse the picture got. In a few weeks, it could threaten the viability of the floor. Our oxygen could leak out through breaks. And orbital photographs show it is getting bigger as it goes westward. The crevice was possibly more than a kilometer wide. This thing was heading right for us and, just like some monster, could swallow us whole.

Chapter 8

A crevice. Damn it. All this work, all this technology beaten by a hole in the ground. I don't know who I was angrier at, the mission planners who should have seen this thing coming in the orbital images they took for months before we came, or just our own damn bad luck.

Well, after all those experts on Earth analyzed the situation—this time paying more attention to their images, I guess—we had another meeting to hear what the ISC's decision was. It wasn't pretty.

We saw a video link from Earth and live messages from the orbiter and each one said the same thing—we were finished.

They said that if we tried to restart the dome somewhere else, it would cost far more than the ISC could raise if we took 10 years. This Asimov would be seen as a big boondoggle, they called it, and nobody wants to throw good money after bad.

"The ISC will send up an evacuation plan in a week. We'll all be home in six months," Bruce said with more somberness than I have ever heard in a space person.

This great, beautiful settlement we had spent so much of our lives building, and gone through so much hell to get built, would just be a big, empty joke.

"It'll be the Spanish armada of space," Liz said. After she explained to me that that was a bunch of expensive ships that were sunk, I thought, no way—I just couldn't accept this. This was too good a project, and, hell, we were just too good a group of people for this to go down as a failure. No way!

That's what I told Bruce, who answered me waving his hands about and talking in that sort of Canadian-Italian accent of his that is even more unusual than Liz's:

"Just wanting this to be better isn't going to help, Kera. We're on the edge of a giant crevice that dwarfs us. I mean if it's a football, we're a Loonie." That's a Canadian dollar coin.

"I appreciate your determination to succeed," he then told me. "I always have. But we've got to concentrate on getting out of here okay. And don't worry about your future. The ISC has said it will pay generous bonuses to us for what we've accomplished. They absolutely see that this is not our fault."

Bonuses. I didn't go to the other side of the sun to get a direct deposit into my bank account. I came here to help start a new world. And I loved what we had built. I wasn't gonna just sit there and watch it die. I mean that roof, those photovoltaic systems, Rosie and Nigel— they were like living beings to me.

Sleep that night was out of the question. I couldn't even sit on my bed. I mean, how could everybody just take this sitting down?

I walked around the dome a few times to try to deal with all this.

"We haven't even seen this crevice," I said to myself. Then it hit me. I had to see this thing that was causing me so much grief—that was wrecking my career. Like heck if I was going to be defeated by something I couldn't even see.

I didn't want to wait to ask Bruce for permission to do an EVA; I knew he would turn me down anyway. Playing by the rules had gotten me this far, but this situation was different. I just had to take things into my own hands.

I walked into an office to get a disc, then over to the airlock, where I inserted it, then typed in some codes to override the monitor—that's the computer that reports what's going on to mission controllers here in Asimov and up in the orbiter.

I got myself into my suit, powered up my life support system, activated the magnetic field and fastened my helmet. I vacated the atmosphere. I used the disc to black out info from the smallest rover we had, then powered it up. After waiting for the video camera that was scanning the area to turn away from the airlock—our night security team could monitor it—I opened the hatch and drove out, looking at screen shots I had called up of the x-rays of the crevice.

I tried to drive fast enough to be out of there by the time the camera scan came back but slow enough not to kick up a lot of dust. I apparently hit just the right speed, 'cause I didn't hear a thing on the radio from the security people. A perfect getaway.

I kept slicing through the dust, keying on that screen shot of the orbital picture till I was right on the edge of the crevice. And there it was, a crack that widened into a split, slanting downward into what looked like the opening of a cave.

It was a real crevice, not some image on a screen. I very slowly drove forward onto the edge of the slant, more nervous with each inch I traveled. When I heard dust start to slide down from under my front wheels, I decided that was far enough.

I shined the high beams into that thing. The light seemed to go forever. Bruce wasn't kidding about how it dwarfed the Asimov.

The opening I looked into was about 10 meters wide, about the width and shape of one of our canisters of the hardening agents we were going to inject into the next dome. What a waste, I thought—all those canisters and roof rolls we were about ready to start rolling out and would never use.

Then it hit me. Thousands of liters of hardening agents that firm up all those chemicals in the roof rolls. Maybe they would firm up the soil. We could put roof chemicals into the crevice's cracks, then pump the hardening agents into them. And just maybe stop the crevice.

I got ready to hit reverse to go tell Bruce this, but I realized, hell, how could we inject all those things into the soil? Those injectors don't have enough force to spray them more than three or four meters. Then, it was another about-face; the soil samplers, those tubes we pull soil out of the ground with, they can go down as far as 15 meters!

Yes! I gave myself a high five, then shifted into reverse to tell Bruce the good news. But instead of going backward, I started going down. The ground under me was sinking and the more I pushed the accelerator the faster it crumbled. I was sliding down and forward into this hole of no return.

I shot my anchor toward the rear. It's a rocket-powered cord with a series of blades that latch you into the ground. It's narrow, but super-reinforced. It's designed to stabilize you in windstorms, not to keep you from falling, so I just had to hope it would work now as I heard it whipping upward and toward the rear with the sound of a basketball going through a nylon net.

The remaining dirt under me started collapsing faster and went rolling into the crevice and I was sliding that way, too, as the cord wasn't yet pulled to full tension. For a second there, I didn't know if that was it for my life, or if that cord would save me. I could see that the anchor was into the ground, but how firmly?

I closed my eyes for a second, then opened them to see the dirt falling faster and faster. I could still see it careening down 50 or 60 meters below. I was heading there, too. This is it, I told myself. Either I'm going down because the cord has come loose or it hasn't been pulled to full length yet. In a second or two, I'll know. I saw Mom and Dad.

Chapter 9

I felt a jerk, like something pulling me backward. That cord was stretched to full tension and the anchor had held—for now. Still, I was dangling by something not designed to hold a rover in the air.

I radioed in a Code 1 emergency—that's life threatening.

"I need a large rover to extract me from the western entrance to the crevice, stat."

The night security man, a guy from Russia, didn't believe it.

"There's no one on an EVA. Where are you?"

So I flipped the override switch off, causing the rover data to come up on his screen.

He said something in Russian, then activated an alarm that everybody on Asimov could hear.

I told him exactly where I was and what had happened.

"Rover crew coming," he said.

I stared down into the gates of hell for five minutes, hoping and praying and wondering if I could jettison parts of that rover. It's just 38 percent G, I kept telling myself. Maybe, this cord will hold.

Finally, I heard a larger, four-person rover coming up behind me.

"I'm about eight meters into the ground with a solid wall behind me that the cord is up against," I told them. That's about 25 feet. "No-go on trying to climb up the cord. It could break."

They then started arguing about whether to try to attach their tow directly to my rover or to the anchor.

"Just do something!" I said. "I'm in real trouble."

In a few seconds, I started to move up, as they had apparently settled on how to tow me. This caused the wall of soil behind me to completely collapse and I was surrounded by dirt, like I was a plow furrowing through the ground. Or a surfer inside a wave. Couldn't see a thing. Couldn't tell whether I was going up or down.

Then, I felt myself being pulled backward, and the soil cleared. I brushed it off my visor and I was up, out of the crevice. They kept pulling me backward, about 20 meters, till they figured I was safe. I thanked the two people in the rescue rover.

Back in the Asimov, I had to deal with Bruce—and the rest of the crew, who had had their sleep interrupted and looked sort of concerned about me, but also confused as hell as to why I was standing there next to a rover absolutely clogged with dust taking off a suit covered with the stuff.

Bruce seemed angry, but also just plain shocked.

"Just what were you doing? You could be expelled from the ISC for this…. Why are you smiling? I'm telling you your career could be over!"

"I've got a way to stop the crevice…."

"What are you talking about? Do you realize that you took a rover and went on an EVA without author… What way to stop the crevice?"

As I told him my idea, he kept bouncing back and forth between being mad over my little trip and fascinated with my suggestion of using roof chemicals in the ground. But that's not to say he was totally big on it.

"How could we use the soil samplers to put chemicals *into* the soil?" he asked. "Their pumps pull soil *out of* the ground."

"We could reverse the pump mechanism," I said, excited enough to have pumped those chemicals into the ground myself. "I know how to do it. I have all the protocols in my computer."

"Yeah, but all this is based on the idea of getting those roof chemicals out of the roof rolls," Bruce added. "I don't know if we can do that. Those rolls are designed to withstand windstorms and meteors. I don't know what we have here that could break them open. The ISC just didn't plan for this."

"Rose and Nigel!" I said. "We can program over 700 tasks into 'em and we can create our own tasks, remember? Just in case we need new ones. Maybe the ISC did plan for this."

Then Bruce, much calmer now, like he was thinking this over—a lot like Collen—leaned back in his seat. Then after a few seconds of silence that had me wondering if my idea was ever gonna be tried, he held his palms out and said: "What have we got to lose?"

"But first we've got to sell mission control on this. I'll tell them about your idea *before* I tell them about you breaking the rules into a million pieces. And I will report that, but—as I said—after we give them the good news. That's not to butter them up, you understand. It's just that we've got to move fast with this plan to stop the crevice, so we need to give them just one thing to think about at a time."

His look, just then, got more stern.

"And I want you to know, this isn't like Star Trek, where they looked the other way because Kirk and the gang brought the whales into the future. You could face very serious punishment."

His voice lowered. "I'm so glad you're okay, Kera."

The next day, before we talked to mission control, we tried to sell this plan to the engineers and scientists there in Asimov. Never mind that I nearly lost my life coming up with it, they kept shooting down the idea of reversing the pumps. I have never been able to get past the idea that the reason was that here they were, the best PhDs in the world—either world—and they were being given a plan by a person who had never been to college. And it was a plan that it was really their job to think up.

Then Bruce asked if I could excuse the six of them, so I left, figuring he was gonna tell them not to worry about being shown up by a technical worker, because this would save the whole project. I don't know if that's what he said, but a half an hour later, he called me back and said they had come up with a plan to start reversing the pumps and mission control gave the okay to test this idea out on a small section of the crevice.

In an hour, I was one of three technical workers and two engineers working on reversing the mechanisms of those pumps. Meanwhile, others broke open a section of roof roll, which turned out not to be as difficult as Bruce had thought. It was like what I guess pressing oil out of olives would be like.

Then, an EVA crew rode out in one of our large rovers—the kind that saved me—to about 70 meters from the eastern side of Asimov. As we listened and wrung our hands, they injected a few liters of roof chemicals into the cracks, then the hardening agents.

They didn't say much after the injections, but while they were in the airlock preparing to re-enter, one of them did a thumbs up. Minutes later, his out-of-breath crew leader told us they had some good results.

"It looks like it seals the cracks," she said. "But exactly what it's gonna do when we use it on the real thing, we don't know. The crevice may just go around our seals."

Another problem she and other engineers had was not knowing how much of these chemicals to use. They weren't designed for anything close to this kind of use. The stuff we had on hand and the next round coming to us by drone would only last so long and of course we still had to use them for the new roofs.

When I would stop and think about what we were doing, spraying roof construction chemicals into the ground—chemicals designed by the best brains on Earth—I'd think, "This is crazy." But then what's crazy when you're on Mars, I thought as I watched the EVA crew take off their radiation resistant electro-magnetized suits—that are the only things that keep them from getting cancer—and start to eat freeze-dried chicken processed 50 million miles away.

Chapter 10

The EVA crews kept applying the chemicals along the western edge of the crevice, then spreading them toward the east away from Asimov. We kept coming up with better ways to make those pumps work based on how things were going out in the soil.

There was no one moment when we all said, "we did it!" Over the next three weeks, we kept sighing relief each time the EVA inspections or orbital images came back and showed the crevice hadn't moved any closer to us.

If things were going well under Mars' surface, we had more reason to worry on the planet where they were paying for all this. The ISC said funding for the rest of the project was getting tight because we would need more chemicals and roof sections—and more time.

We were months behind schedule in raising the next roof and we would need more time still to be sure this crevice stopping plan would work before we could even think of raising it.

During a meeting about the Asimov's finances, I learned two new words: patent receipts.

It turned out that the ISC had been splitting revenue from things or processes that had been developed on Nova. Private companies made them, but they needed the zero G of the station's central bay to make them in. So they agreed to give the ISC half the money they earned from selling the rights to them, since it was us who made the zero-G possible.

Now we were dipping into the patent receipts to help keep us going. I never knew that all those years on Nova, I was working for a business. That was years ago in Earth orbit. Today, before we could earn any more patent receipts, we had to plug the crevice, and the images and ground inspections kept looking good.

The crevice's main section was stopped cold; it wasn't moving toward us and the tentacles under our eastern side were actually receding.

Because of this good news, and the need to keep the donors giving, the ISC made us do one of my least favorite things. Yeah, you guessed it. We gave an interview to media all over Earth. And yes, the ISC gave them my name as the person who thought up the injection method of stopping the crevice.

"We all deserve the credit," I said after a reporter asked if I wasn't the most important member of the crew for coming up with the idea. "We're a team. We all help each other out and many people made the pumps and roof chemicals work. That's people here—the scientists, the engineers, the technical workers—and a lot of Nerva and ground support people, too."

That was really how I felt. I wasn't just saying that to sound right. But after the interview, I could see right away that some of the PhDs were relieved that I gave them some of the credit.

More of them smiled at me than I had ever seen smile at once and an American engineer who had worked with NASA during the Space Shuttle days gave me a high-five and said, "You are a steely-eyed missile woman."

That's the best thing you can say about someone in space. It means someone who really uses their head to come up with a solution to a tough problem. For an engineer to say that to a non-engineer is really something.

And, I won't kid you, for a man who is an engineer to say that about someone he knew was a lesbian was a good thing, too.

So with everybody in the ISC knowing how important I had been in saving us from the crevice, Bruce figured now was the time to report me for my late night jaunt.

First, I e-mailed a statement, admitting what I did and saying why I did it. The ISC assigned a "Personnel Policy Representative" to my case, a crew member who made sure the rules were followed and my rights weren't violated. He was the closest thing we had to a lawyer on Mars.

I then saw a "live" message from the ISC office in Houston, where this woman in charge of promotions and personnel said it looked like a clear case of disobedience, but that my heroics with the crevice might carry some weight with them when they decided on my punishment. That could include being taken off duty and being brought back, maybe even in detention.

Detention itself wouldn't be that much tougher than being on the Nerva anyway, but that word—detention—it sounded awful, like I was some kind of juvenile offender. The offender part, sure, I admitted I had been that. But juvenile, geez.

Then the camera in Houston panned over to her assistant and he said punishment wouldn't be given out till after the Christmas holiday. He said several more things over the next five minutes about the procedures that would be followed.

I didn't hear any of that, because of something that happened for a split second during the camera pan. I could see out the window there in Houston a patch of blue sky and a white cloud or two.

It was just a flash, and it was a tiny part of the screen, but I was now wishing I hadn't seen it at all. That blue and that puffy cloud there in Texas in December—it looked like spring in Louisville.

Well, after I came out of that video session, Liz and the personnel guy, a Korean computer engineer named Jae-Sun, asked me all kinds of questions about what was said. I knew it was because Liz cared about me and Jae-Sun was doing his job, but it got tiring.

"Yes, they said I could get detention," I told them. "I don't really remember much of what they said after that sky. I mean after that *statement*. Look, I'm tired. Can we wait till later to talk about this?"

But they both said, no, we've got to fight for your rights and right now. They were so pumped, so raring to go. And I was so out of it.

"Please," I said. "They're not going to do anything till after the holiday, so can't we just wait till then to talk about it?" Sorry Liz and Jae-Sun, but that little patch of sky just wouldn't let go of me.

A couple of days later, I looked around while I was on an EVA and realized that for all the excitement over being the first on Mars, this was a flat, sandy region that all looked the same as far as we could see in any direction.

"Another day on Aacidalia Planitia," I mumbled. I realized that every time I or somebody else said that, it sounded more and more glum.

Sure, it was a thrill to have come here, but when I looked at the orbital photos of the mountainous places future expeditions would go, I felt a little cheated. Those missions would use Asimov for a staging area, then go to places where the landforms and even the colors are different—yes, there are places on Mars that have blue and white patches and lots of hills. And let's not forget the polar expeditions and the ones to volcanoes.

As great an opportunity as it was to be the first to come to Mars, we were just the table setters for much more involved missions. That's the way space is. If you're first somewhere, the people who follow you make your work look primitive.

Well, once the ISC figured the crevice had been stopped, we received more roof supplies. Then we had to get to work catching up on our schedule. But soon we got a day off. For you on Earth, it was Dec. 25. It was our first Christmas on Mars, but if there was one thing we didn't need, it was a guy in a red suit—with a red-nosed reindeer.

Anything but more red—even if Christmas red is rosy red, compared to the rusty red we saw everywhere. At least we had a green tree, although it was artificial. Just to see something that *looked* like it was on Earth was something else. The tree, plus all the grain and crops we were growing in aerated soil made me realize how much of a desert we were surrounded by.

At least it was Christmas. The strange thing about the holiday in Asimov was that those of us from Christian countries mostly weren't religious; at least we didn't belong to any church. There were three of the crew who were from Moslem countries and they were very much into their Islamic faith. One of them, this very nice woman named Merit, who was from Egypt but who had lived in Chicago for years, told me all about Christianity in Africa before it moved to Europe.

She taught me a lot about the church I grew up in—that I was wrong to think the only Christians in Africa were because of missionaries from our part of the world. The church I attended as a girl always talked about how we were saving souls in Africa by sending missionaries.

Merit told me there were three African popes before the year 500 A.D. I never would have guessed that.

It was also great to see that these Moslem folks not only knew a lot about Christianity, they were very warm toward it. It wasn't like you'd think from all the news stories about Moslem terrorists and all that.

The most devout Christian I knew at Asimov was an electrical engineer from Tanzania named Anza. He was about 50 and very athletic and thin. He loved running and you would always see him lapping the interior of the colony. His long legs would have made big strides even on Earth, so you can imagine how much territory they covered in Mars gravity.

Anza was named for the headmaster of the Lutheran school where his parents went. That gives you an idea of how big the Lutheran Church was in his life.

It's called the Evangelical Lutheran Church in Tanzania. He showed me lots of video streams about the church and life in Tanzania and it gave me a feeling I hadn't had since high school, when I first went to a black community in Louisville.

Just like back then, it was two feelings in one—one was great, because I understood Africa better. The other was, well, lousy, because I now understood how wrong it was of me to think that an African country couldn't have all the things Tanzania did.

I guess I had grown up seeing Africans as hopeless, poor, hungry and killing each other or dying of AIDS. And, yes, Anza said those things happen—it was scary how many people in Tanzania he said had AIDS—but he said normal life happens there, too. Tanzania had churches, mosques, schools, businesses, and farms galore. I mean learning about how their farm economy works from Anza and those video streams was one of the things that got me interested in farming here.

He showed me Africans who were, well, taking care of themselves.

"Unfortunately, the television and news streams usually show Africa as all chaos and misery and filled with vices," Anza told me. "That is because the media go into African nations with a lot of stereotypes. They just won't show the good side."

His voice was soft and pleasing, not at all angry, even though he was criticizing our part of the world. And that word "stereotypes" was a word I knew well, from my many years in lesbian feminism.

I remember from the video streams how busy the marketplaces were in Tanzanian cities, especially Dar es Salaam, the biggest city—everybody trying to sell their produce and clothing and other things. It really looked organized.

Some of the other numbers, besides the scary ones about AIDS, made me remember a discussion Paula, Amy and I had about whether feminism really matters in poor countries like in Africa. Sometimes, people say, no, they are all so oppressed, the men as much as the women, that our feminist ideals don't really matter—that it's just plain liberation they need, not women's liberation, as I heard one person put it once.

Not true, according to some figures about Tanzania I found on a stream after talking to Anza. Women were a lot more likely than men to be poor there, to not know how to read and to have AIDS.

Yep, feminism matters in Africa more than I thought—maybe even more than Paula and Amy thought.

Anza said something else about his country that sent me back to my computer. When I mentioned that this part of Acidalia Planitia was as flat as Kansas and as sandy as the Mohave Desert—two places I had driven through several times when I was an equipment installer—he said: "It reminds me of the Serengeti."

He told me that comes from the word for "endless plains" in the language of the Maasai, the people who live near there. I immediately started calling up videos of the Serengeti, which is in Tanzania and Kenya. Wow, what a sensational spot—mountains, wildlife like I'd never seen and, just like he said, this beautiful plain.

I loved those videos of wildebeests and zebras migrating. Learning about the Serengeti and farming in Tanzania has Maria and me saving our money for a trip there in a few years. Anza said our family can stay with his. Can't wait.

But I think I got more into Tanzania from how seriously Anza took the Christmas celebration. It wasn't about presents and jingle bells. It was about Jesus. And even though I'm never gonna be into a strict faith—I've seen too many people twist Jesus into gay hating—it was really nice seeing the real meaning of Christianity, not all the stuff we are raised to think Christmas is about. Maybe it took someone from another part of Earth to make that clear to me.

So it was a great Christmas. It was also good hearing from everyone I had sent e-mail cards to, but then I got the shock of my life. Paula e-mailed me back with news that just ruined it. She and Amy had broken up.

The best couple I had ever known. They were the way I wanted to be if I ever married somebody. I mean the way they laughed at everything, the way they disagreed about things and stayed so happy. I wanted to jump right onto a shuttle and go straight to Bremen and tell them, stop this nonsense and get back together!

Then I read the rest of Paula's e-mail and I realized they had to do what was right for them. They had "just grown apart," Paula said. They had no fights, they just realized that "the enjoyment of life requires us to no longer be intimate partners," Paula wrote. I'll never forget they way she put that.

She said they'd stay occasional friends. That I figured, because they had both told me that lesbian feminism is the smallest village you'll ever live in. Your girlfriend is your best friend's ex-girlfriend. Your ex-girlfriend is in charge of your next political rally and so on.

But damn that hurt.

I decided to cope by burying myself in my work. And with new supplies arriving, and our second round of crew members due in four months, we built and we built and we built. First, the new roof. Then more residences, an auditorium, a communications center, a larger plant and food processing facility and of course more of the black and grey corridors.

Two days into the new Earth year, Bruce called me into his office and I knew right away what the reason was. Yep, the ISC had decided what action to take against me for borrowing the car without permission. And it wasn't grounding me for the weekend and no beer at the school dance.

I still have the printout filed away in a desk drawer, just to remind me never to pull something like that again, as though remembering the terror of staring down into the abyss for five minutes wouldn't do the job.

There I was, Kera McLain, the top robotics and construction person in the ISC, in "administrative detention." They offered me two types of punishment, then—and this is just like the ISC—they made it so I could only chose the one they wanted me to.

I was relieved of my Asimov duties and ordered back to Earth, but I could also voluntarily put in for return and they would keep the punishment private and let me keep working till I left. You see, they also said if I didn't come voluntarily, they would release all the details of my case to the news media, so everybody I have ever met would know I had messed up.

Well you know me and news coverage. I don't mind telling you now because of all the years that have passed. But back then, the thought of being in the news made it an easy decision to voluntarily put in for return.

That didn't sit well with Liz or Jae-Sun, my personnel guy.

"We can appeal this and we can win, because of your stopping the crevice!" Liz said, all juiced up like she had been last month when we last talked about this.

"And your work record is outstanding, a real model, until the EVA," Jae-Sun said. He then called up the appeal form on his screen and started to print it out.

"Hold it," I said. "First of all, I did break the rules by taking the rover. And besides…"

"No Kera!" Liz said. "I can't believe I'm hearing you saying that. We've got to fight them all the way on this. It just isn't fair to treat you this way. We've got to be brave."

"Don't tell me about being brave!" I said. "I stared death in the face and almost lost to it--while you were snug in your bed all packed to come home! Now you're telling me I don't know how to fight? Besides, all you two are worried about is your batting average."

I walked out and rested in my room about an hour, then called Liz. We met in a conference room.

"I yelled at the best friend I've got on Mars, maybe Earth, too. I'm sorry Liz."

"No problem," she said real softly while she patted me on the arm. "Only you know what's right for you. Maybe we were a little concerned about ourselves."

"Well, I was way out of line to say what I did. I hate the way I came across, like I'm better than other people because I thought of the plan. Geez, how could I have said that to you? And after I was so modest in the interview, giving credit to everybody."

"You had a little bout with being human and that's okay."

I smiled while I thought of all we used to talk about on the TMSO.

"I guess if we can make God and the evolutionists agree, we can put our differences aside," I said.

I talked to Jae-Sun at supper that night and told him I was sorry for the blowup. He took it well, but what neither of the two of them could understand, and what it took me a little while to understand, too, was what all this started over. And that was the fact that I was a little embarrassed that I suddenly wanted to give all this up—I mean the greatest construction project human beings have ever tried, the greatest adventure in history—because of a little picture of sky.

And I lashed out at Liz—and everybody else on Asimov—because of feeling so lousy over that patch of blue and the power it had over me. I was such a space woman, but now I wanted to see blue sky—I mean more than a few minutes a day during the Martian sunset when blue and purple are visible above the horizon.

I started looking forward every day to sunsets just for the chance to see some blue. And that made me want to see it all day. Even grey cloudy skies would be okay. For that matter, I wanted outside to be a place that wasn't full of poison and a place I could go without 30 minutes of preparation.

I wanted a home and a wife, if the right woman should come by. I wanted every day to be simple, same-ole' things.

Yep, my mood was different from when I finished up my two years on Nova. Back then, all I wanted was to stay in space. Earth just offered me nothing.

Far from being pulled kicking and screaming, I couldn't wait for the ISC to schedule our return. But here's the thing: because of the position of the planets, I couldn't come home till spring, which was probably about the time I would have been scheduled for a return anyway. So my punishment wasn't much of a penalty.

Instead of feeling bad about it, I actually wondered how I could speed up my return. Maybe I should do a TV interview about how much I loved it in Asimov, then talk to a psychiatrist—that got me home early last time.

I can smile now when I remember how I thought that—you see my service on Nova came to an end after I did two interviews really talking up life on the station. The ground folks thought I liked it too much, so they had a psychiatrist examine me, and she told them they should bring me down because I wasn't so well adjusted on Earth.

What a difference. Then, I was about 60 minutes from being on the ground and desperately wanted to stay off of it. This time, I just had to get home to Earth, but it would be a year before I could. Back then, I wondered if I could survive being back on Earth. Now, I was shaking in my bed some nights wondering how in God's name I would survive until I got back to it.

Chapter 11

We were catching up on our building, and with the construction schedule lighter, the crevice stopped and the dust storms coming soon, I got my formal orders to come home. It would be spring when I left Mars, then about six months of a return trip inside that lead dungeon–yes, you can see I was souring on long distance space travel, compared to my early days.

Don't get me wrong—it was still a fantastic thing to have gotten to serve in space and to go to places so few people will ever get to go. I am very proud of everything I accomplished and I love the people I worked closely with.

But I was just dying to get back during the rest of that Earth winter, and the next spring I just had to, because here came those dust storms. I realized for the first time just how cut off we were. The dust made a sizzling noise as it rifled over the dome day and night.

Good God, I thought several times, that stuff is never gonna quit. You'd just keep thinking, okay, that's enough, now stop. But it wouldn't. It went on for a month of non-stop noise. And that dome conducted the sound so well, you could hear it, almost feel it, day and night. I'd listen to music or watch videos just to try to cover up the sound, but it was everywhere.

"The dome is functioning well," Bruce told us at a meeting. "So far, we don't need any exterior repairs by robot. The noise, unfortunately, is something we can't reduce."

I was usually quiet during those meetings, but I just had to chime in: "It's like living underneath a grill with bratwursts cooking on it." I wish I hadn't said that, because it made me hungry for a juicy brat and that made me suddenly realize how plain the food was on Asimov.

Later that day, I found out I wasn't the only one feeling that way.

"Thanks a lot for mentioning bratwursts," an American construction worker said while stirring his freeze-dried peas in the dining hall. "That's all I can think about when I hear that noise, which is all day."

"Sorry," I said. "It hit me too. I guess we get the sound of brats, but not the taste."

It wasn't just our tongues that were hurting. The all-day dust cloud out there reduced our solar electricity supply by 70 percent. We had enough stored in batteries—and being made by fuel cells—to get by, but after one week of the storm, we had to limit listening to music and watching videos at night, which made it even harder to get that damn noise out of our heads.

At least I really appreciated how well made the dome was because it was taking a pounding. But at the same time, this storm made me doubt that people could ever live here. I mean live a decent life.

Some people on Earth in the ISC and other organizations want to do what they call "transmogrifying" the Martian atmosphere by adding new gases so that in about 120 years or so it could support grass, shrubs and then people—breathing on our own, not with life support. The sky would even be blue if we pulled that off.

Well, I was big on this idea for a while, thinking we were paving the way for making Mars like Earth. But if they're reading this, my message since the storm is: hold on. Sure, transmogrifying is a great idea, but unless you can tame that dust, count me out, or count my great-great-grandchildren out.

To ride the storm out, I kept doing construction and maintenance on the place, trying not to think about how long it was till I would start for home. Then, over three days, the storm eased up, then stopped. Man, it was quiet out there.

Our sensors showed the dome had held up well, but, using the robots, we put a new outer layer of lead on it. I made a few more EVAs for that and it was great to get outside, to see a sky, even a red one. It did make me realize how beautiful Mars is. I hope we don't spoil it someday by building so much stuff there that it starts to look like Arizona or California—full of subdivisions and shopping centers.

The storms had turned the soil even more crumbly than it had been. Now that we had gotten the Asimov up and running, the scientists would start doing experiments to find any evidence of life on Mars.

They'd soon start heading out on expeditions to look for chemical evidence of simple life forms or, and this was the big deal that had everybody excited, they'd use sonar to look for underground remains of civilizations.

That's another story, of course, and your paper has already written about that.

I was thinkin' more about life on Earth—mine. And as it got closer to the day to lift off, coming home was *all* I could think about. We had a little reception at lunch for the seven of us leaving and I figured that was all there would be before I left three days later in the drone MEM that had landed.

Then, the next day, Bruce called me over the PA system to the dining hall. Strangely, everybody else was going there too. I looked in and saw a sign that explained why.

It said: "Kera McLain, Once and Future Earthling." It was a dinner in my honor.

"This is great of you guys," I told everybody.

"Well, you might not say that if you knew what kind of an event this is," Liz said. "It's a roast."

Yep, I was the guest of honor. I still have the scripts they used.

Bruce got up to the microphone.

"You may recall that when we first proposed the Asimov project, the money was very slow in coming. So we stressed the chance to create a new livable environment for the human race, but the money still barely

came in at all. Then we said it will create jobs all over the world, but the money was still just a trickle. Then finally we said this project will get Kera McLain to leave the Earth, and look at us now—we're rolling in dough."

"That's probably true," I said while laughing myself silly.

Then, Liz got up there and as she grinned at me I thought, my God, what could she be about to say?

"Kera and I are proof lesbians aren't man haters. The kinship between us all here, the years of bonding in training, the shared belief in our mission all show how much we love and respect the men we work with. Besides, they could cut off our oxygen during our EVAs if we let 'em know how we really felt."

"No, No!" I shrieked while waving my hands back and forth. But let me tell you, it's hard to be heard over almost every person in Asimov—that is almost every person *in the world*—laughing in that dining hall.

I noticed that Anza was laughing, too—a lot, leaning his high forehead back and clapping his hands. He had always been so soft-spoken that I couldn't have imagined him doing big belly laughs till I saw him doing it then.

What a night. When it was finally my turn to talk, I just took the microphone and said: "You folks are funny. You sure *you're* not the gay ones?"

Everybody laughed even louder, including Anza. That was a pretty good sign that he wasn't homophobic, despite being from a traditional church. He had never said anything homophobic at all, but I had always avoided the subject. Now, well, he looked like anything but the uptight person a homophobe would be.

There was one more EVA, the walk to the MEM for the launch. It was sad to leave Asimov for the last time ever, even more than leaving Nova, 'cause then I knew I might be back someday. And as I walked on the surface and looked at that red sky, something occurred to me for the first time. I wondered, what is *nature*?

I mean the environmentalists on Earth, the religions, the schools—they all talk about how we have to take care of the planet. I heard it all the time growing up. They all said this was the only moral thing to do because we were part of nature.

But is this place, Mars, nature, too? Could we dump our trash all over here and pour soot into the air out of smokestacks without committing a crime against nature?

Yes, I had been so busy during my time on Mars with all the construction and the crevice that I didn't really get to think about this until my last few hours on the planet.

And as I saw the surface getting smaller and smaller during that lift off, I remember asking myself, is that nature down there? After I got back to the orbiter and looked down at the planet, I not only asked myself that, but also, what is God?

The next day, after we were settled into the orbiter, I talked about this with Anza, my favorite Christian in the crew, who had lifted off with my group.

I didn't know how he'd feel about me suggesting that the Bible was not complete because it talks only about the Earth as a place where life is. As far as my belief that the only real God isn't just a Christian one, forget it, I didn't even want to get into that.

Well, Anza surprised me. He told me the Old Testament has references to Jupiter and Venus, which looked like stars to folks back then. But he also said there was no reference to life anywhere but Earth.

"I am a man of science who has lived on two planets," he said. "I am also a man of God who seeks eternal life through Jesus Christ. As far as whether our search for life on Mars strays from the Bible, I'm reminded of the words of Jesus in Matthew: 'O thou of little faith, wherefore didst thou doubt?' If we use the minds God gave us to explore, we'll only find His truth—whatever is actually out there. I have no doubt."

I thought a lot about what he said. Still do. And I decided to tell Collen by e-mail about all this thinking I was doing about God and the universe. And Collen said that what I was feeling, believe it or not, was a victory for the Asimov project.

"Our biggest goal was to expand thinking," he e-mailed me. "And what you have said about Martian nature and God indicates we are doing that." Then he asked my permission to use what I had said in a presentation he was going to do in Sweden in a month. No problem, I said. I mean I owed him a million favors.

In the orbiter, getting used to zero-g again was tough, even though I could use the Ag an hour a day. But it was mostly weightless living and the return trip would be five and a half months.

Five and a half months. I liked to think of it as 165 days—somehow that didn't sound as long.

We didn't have any landing or construction coming up, so it wasn't at all like the trip out there with so much to look forward to. We were just sitting inside a tin can.

Suddenly, I was not so cool on something that didn't bother me at all during the early days of the project. That was the slight chance—a "slightly elevated risk," they called it—that I could get cancer from the small amounts of high radiation that might have gotten through the lead coating on the ships and the Asimov.

What the hell was I thinking when I agreed to that? Sure, risk was what space travel was all about, but today, my children and Maria are what my life is all about and.... Well, let's not talk about that. Every checkup so far shows that I am fine.

The trip back—the first sign that we were getting closer was when the Earth looked the same size as Mars. But that's tricky, because that meant we were just one-third the way home because of the size of the planets.

But as we got closer, we could start to see more detail without a telescope. First the polar regions, then—and this was so wonderful, I cried—some blue color! I'd look on the monitor by the hour at the Earth.

And when it got big enough so I could see some land as well as ocean, I had another one of those deep moments I had plenty of on this mission. I looked at that tiny little ball in this giant black sea and I thought, wow, how fragile it is, the Earth.

Everything that has ever happened to the human race, except space exploration, has happened in that tiny circle the size of a golf ball at about 40 or 50 meters away. Stop fighting over it, people. If you could see it like this, you'd all stop making war forever. And stop polluting it! It's all we've got.

The TESO wasn't all deep thoughts, though. That's the Trans-Earth Solar Orbit—the trip home. They showed us some old movies about trips to Mars, and wars between us and the Martians that were supposed to live there.

Some of them were serious, some so silly—including one about Santa Claus being kidnapped by Martians. *Really.* I guess it says how bored we were most of the trip that I even watched *that* one.

I don't know why the ISC showed 'em to us—maybe to show how long people have been thinkin' about going to Mars, or maybe it was just that somebody in the organization had a sense of humor. Collen, I'll bet.

Chapter 12

Even with the movies, the e-mails and the Earth constantly gettin' bigger, the five months of the TESO were slow. It reminded me of being in an isolation booth for 24 hours as part of my Nova training. You just wanted to push the ship along. At least on a *real* ship, I mean on an ocean, you could grab an oar and row.

Finally, we were e-mailed the itinerary for our return: A day and a half on good ole' Nova, then a shuttle to KSC—that's the Kennedy Space Center—where we'd meet our families, then go through three weeks of testing and de-briefing before we could get out to all that blue sky I was craving so much.

I couldn't believe the way they treated us on Nova—like we were Martians coming to Earth for the first time. "I just want to be an Earthling again," I said several times. I was so tired. I mean mentally and physically. All that praise they heaped on me, all those looks I got from everybody, like I was some kind of god, that all meant nothing.

But after we landed, seeing Mom and Dad and my sister Terri and her family—that meant everything. Dad kept saying "that's alright, dear, you don't have to tell them anything" when the reporters kept demanding I answer their questions.

When I was a kid, he would say things like that to shelter me 'cause he was such a fearful person. But this time, it was different. I felt Dad really understood me and was on my side. I was just so overwhelmed with feelings, and strange new sights and one-G all the time that I didn't know what to say to anybody.

Then I saw something on a video screen there at KSC that just said it all. It was a magazine cover with some of us on Mars. It said: "Bringing Worlds Together."

Those words ended Kera's narrative. She repeated: "Bringing Worlds Together," flashing a look of acknowledgement of a double-meaning concerning the great distance that had separated her from relatives for much of her life.

The two journalists took the statement as a cue that it was time to end the interview and start mentally processing what they had heard in advance of transcribing and transmitting the story of the first trip to Mars told in a decidedly and heretofore unheard grassroots way.

Kera and Maria didn't know it, but the word "book" danced in front of Julian Ross' eyes as he realized more than ever that a single news story, no matter how extensive, could not contain what Kera had just told him.

Several times during the interview, his eyes had met the videographer's in moments of realization that this indeed was a giant story that could bring them both rewards, assuming they went about proposing a book deal gradually so as not to upset a good relationship with such a highly private source.

Kera's ambitions were not of personal gain, but were hardly modest either. As she had said, hastening the acceptance of same-sex marriage in her homeland was a prime motive for this uncharacteristically public and candid presentation.

And as the midday sun finished drying the dew off the peppers behind the house, Kera and Maria did a little semi-staged tending to the crops to give the videographer some good images while the children struggled to seem oblivious to her cameras as they played nearby.

Back in the house, amid some feelings of self-consciousness over all she had revealed to these strangers, Kera, along with her family, wished farewell to Julian and Jessica, who left for their familiar, more urban cove of New Zealand's creative class.

Minutes later, Kera and Maria, seated on the back porch, watched their children manipulate the controls of their got-to-have cyber games, framed by rows of the kiwifruits and peppers the couple would soon pick and transport to market.

As the call of a bird in a grove of trees behind the farm wafted on the breeze that glided by Kera's face, she suddenly was aware of a circular quality of her life. The sensations were straight from the quiet working class neighborhoods where she had spent her childhood in the middle of North America before being pulled so far afield.

After a few seconds, Kera pulled out her phone pod to check for calls that might have come in during the interview. Seeing none, she grinned slightly as she wondered while glancing skyward who perhaps at that very moment was doing her old job of maintaining the satellite that made this ultimate 21st century consumer device usable.

What a shame it would be to waste their efforts, Kera decided as she pressed a memory key.

"Hello, Mom?"

The End